Herman Mertens

The lost German U-boat

novum ◣ pro

This book is also available as e-book.

www.novum-publishing.co.uk

© 2023 novum publishing

ISBN 978-3-99131-434-9
Editing: Rod Pritchard-Smith
Cover photos: Alinamd,
Carsten Medom Madsen,
Chrisp543 | Dreamstime.com
Cover design, layout & typesetting:
novum publishing

www.novum-publishing.co.uk

Climate neutral
Print product
ClimatePartner.com/16547-2201-1002

Early April 1943, and there are two submarines, U1001 and U1002, in the base of Brest.

Both of them are being subjected to thorough maintenance. After two weeks these boats will be released and will end up in a different dock where each vessel will receive their own cargo.

There is a lot of movement around these two submarines, with much supervision from the SS and the Gestapo. Even Admiral Dönitz was present.

The U1001 was being loaded by the SS and sailors; what the cargo was, no one from the crew knew.

The U1002 was also loaded, but with torpedoes, ammunition and supplies while the 1001 did not receive many torpedoes but had to make do with six.

On Tuesday, April 20th, the signal 'boats loaded and ready for departure' came. Dönitz received both captains for a briefing on Wednesday, April 21st, 1943.

He informed them that they had to leave on April 22nd at four in the morning with a 45-minute time difference between the two departures.

The next morning:

Brest, Thursday April 22nd, 1943: at four o'clock in the morning a U-boat leaves on a secret mission on the direct command of Adolf Hitler, 45 minutes later a second U-boat departs to protect the first, also on Hitler's direct orders.

The first officer reports to the captain: "Boat ready to go Captain."

Then the first order follows: "Start the engines", and the diesels come to life with a cloud of smoke and they spit out even more smoke, then the second order follows: "Bunches loose."

The U-boat slowly disengages from the quay and glides gently through the water towards the open sea.

The captain stands in the tower, looks around, addresses his first mate and says: "Frits, we have left for a few months, I am curious what awaits us."

Frits was lost in thought and did not hear the captain; he was gazing at the horizon watching how dawn broke the night.

A gentle southerly wind was blowing through their hair as the sea lapped quietly. Together they stared through their binoculars scanning in each direction, looking for the enemy.

But everything was quiet and they enjoyed the view.

The captain on the first submarine, U1001, is an officer who was already on a submarine back in the First World War.

Slowly the U1001 glides further through the water towards an unknown adventure. Once on the high seas he prepares to open his orders, as instructed. Karl Heinz Jung, the captain of U1001, gathers his officers in the galley. Once they are all present, he begins to read the Führers commands to his officers:

"Captain, this mission is for the greater good of the German People and must succeed.

Here are the coordinates to follow, they take us towards Brazil.

The U1001 is loaded with very important items that should not fall into enemy hands.

I expect you to complete this assignment according to my wishes.

I wish you the best of luck for this assignment.

Sieg heil

Adolf Hitler

After the first day the captain decides to let the crew practice on a quick dive. He sounds the alarm and gives the orders to dive on the on-board radio. Simultaneously he records the time. After a tumultuous 1 minute and 26 seconds the submarine is fully underwater.

The captain calls his first officer and tells him that the diving must be much faster, this must be done within 35 seconds, that's the guideline. He informs the crew and tells them it's a matter of life or death.

The following days they keep repeating the same exercise and each time the diving speed increases and the time gets better. Until the day they dive under 35 seconds.

"Captain, in today's diving exercise we recorded a time of 33 seconds."

"Thank you, first officer."

A few hours later the captain makes a statement via the ship's intercom:

"This is a message for the entire crew. Gentlemen, as we are getting better and better at doing the exercises to dive faster and faster and we have come to a time of 33 seconds, I wish to express my gratitude for the commitment of all of you. And therefore gentlemen, we are going to choose an uninhabited island where we go ashore. A four-man watch remains on board to guard the boat. Our chefs will go ashore as well and together with some sailors they will hunt for fresh meat, which they will then prepare on the spit."

The captain then proceeded to the officer in charge of the navigation.

"Lieutenant Wemmels."

"Jawohl Captain!"

"Show me our current position on the map so that we can locate an island."

The lieutenant showed the captain where they were on the map:

"Captain, between Funchal and Santa Cruz is an unknown island, we can go there."

"All right, we're going there; what course should we take and how long before we get there?"

"I'll take care of everything, captain, but we'll reach that spot after eight days."

"Okay, inform the crew too."

After a smooth seven-day journey, the message came:

"Land in sight. Captain requested on deck."

The captain made his way to the tower and went on deck.

"Captain, look there is the island."

Together they took their binoculars and viewed the island.

"Find a place where we can moor the U-boat without it being clearly visible from the open seas."

"All right Captain."

After a few hours they had found a suitable place on a large inlet and the U-boat moored there. A landing unit went ashore with the order to bring back branches and bushes so that they could cloak the submarine and make it hard to be discovered.

After a few hours the Germans returned with the necessary things to camouflage the boat.

"Captain for radio operator."

"Operator listening to captain."

"Send message to U1002 with our location so that they can come alongside."

"All right Captain."

Then, over submarine's intercom system came: "This is the captain speaking. Men, we are moored onto an uninhabited island in order to recover for a few days. We will disembark and a four-man watch will remain on board; these four will be switched tomorrow. Everyone has to be equipped with their gun, and for the chef: you go with two sailors to provide fresh meat." Thus, the crew left for the island in rubber dinghies.

The island had alternating sandy and rocky beaches with a dense vegetation of plants.

Everyone started on their assigned tasks. The chef went on a hunt for fresh meat with two sailors. They started their search along the beach. After an hour of walking, a maiden said: "Look here: tracks in the sand and they're heading towards the center of the island, let's follow these tracks."

On their way they passed all kinds of plants. about "Men, wait a minute, these are wild herbs and I can use them well when preparing the meat," the chef said.

Together they started to pick the herbs and put them in a big bag.

They soon entered the bushes and had to clear their way with machetes. The jungle grew thicker and thicker until they suddenly came out on a plain. They quickly dropped onto the grass and looked around with their binoculars until the chef said:

"Men, look there, there is movement at 13 o'clock."

The sailors looked and saw something moving.

"Come on, we're going upwind, so that the animals can't smell us and we can get close enough to see what kind of animals they are. No sooner said than done, they went around and against the wind to the spot the chef had indicated. At a good thirty-meter distance, they could hear the animals. They made a grunting sound.

"Men, I think it's wild pigs," the chef said. They sneaked closer and indeed they were pigs but not wild, they were feral pigs roaming around.

A sailor took out his weapon, a mauser.

"Which one should I shoot?" he asked.

"I see some sows over there. Shoot one of those pigs and let those sows live."

The sailor steadied his sights and a shot was heard. The pig slumped through his legs and lay dead on the ground. Because of the noise the other pigs had all started to move off.

The sailors chopped off some sturdy branches and made a frame to tie the pig onto so they could head back to the beach.

Meanwhile, the crew was preparing a fire behind a small ridge so that the flames would not be visible from the sea.

Other sailors had also set out to find fruit and edible plants. They had also found what they were looking for and brought bananas, pineapples, coconuts and other fruits. They had also come across a half-decayed cabin with alongside it a lost vegetable garden, where they found all kinds of vegetables, such as cabbages, tomatoes, potatoes and much more, that grew in the wild garden. But on looking into the remains of the cabin, they found a human skeleton.

They immediately decided to search around the rest of the area of the cabin to see if they could find anything else. Sure enough, a good fifty meters behind it was a small hillock completely enclosed by thickets. After cutting down parts of the bush, an entrance to a cave emerged.

The men looked at each other and after making torches, entered. Once inside, they were amazed at what they saw. It had been the pirate's pantry. Inside were chests containing all sorts of items – clothes, pewter cups, pistols, some kegs with gunpowder and two barrels of rum.

Then the non-commissioned officer said:

"We are going to report this to the captain first and he will then tell us what to do with it. But for now, let's take a barrel of rum with us."

The men headed back to the beach and once there, informed the captain.

"We leave everything as it is," he said. But I will write everything about this island down in my diary for when we return to it later. But first I want to execute my orders further."

The chef went to the captain and asked: "How do you want me to prepare the pig?"

"Is that possible on a spit?" the captain replied.

"Yes, of course, but then it will take a while before we can eat."

"No problem", said the captain. "We have plenty of time and rum, just get started."

They slaughtered the pig and removed its organs. The chef took the pig's intestines and prepared them to make sausages. Then the pig was spit-laced and seasoned, and the fire was lit at the same time. Once that was done, they started grilling the pig. The chef also prepared dishes from all the fruit and vegetables they had collected.

Simultaneously, he started making the sausages which he would later smoke, so they could be stored for a longer time.

Meanwhile U1002 had come alongside and they had also camouflaged their boat. The U1002 captain made landfall and was treated to a cup of rum. Both captains clinked glasses and drank heartily.

After a few hours, the meal was ready and everyone got their part of the food. The men enjoyed their meal and later they all scattered themselves around, each finding a place to enjoy the sun and the view.

The next day the crew was switched and they also were presented with the same meal. And they too thoroughly enjoyed their drinks and food.

After four days, both captains decided to continue sailing and carry out their Führer's orders. The crew was well-rested and full of energy to carry out their mission.

The U1001 left towards Little San Salvador and 45 minutes after, the U1002 followed suit. Once again they practiced fast diving and each time they reached the pre-set time.

The journey was then continued above water. The captain and some officers kept a lookout and scanned the horizon for enemy ships. Everything was quiet but then, after a 28-day journey, the alarm suddenly sounds. "**SONAR TO CAPTAIN!!**"

"Captain's listening."

"I hear propellers from a ship."

"How far away from us?"

"Captain, about a thousand meters."

"Dive, dive, dive."

Now the crew understood the many exercises of the past few days and after 35 seconds they disappeared below the surface. Complete silence on board and enter combat mode. "Sonar, where's the enemy?"

"Captain, he has turned around and started the chase."

"Dive down to 100 meters and look for a cold layer of water, their sonar cannot detect us under that."

A total silence.

"Captain, we are under a cold layer but it is moving quickly."

"Try to follow this so we stay out of the picture."

"Captain, we are losing the layer!"

Complete silence now!

"Captain, he's checking for us." (ping, ping, ping, ping, pong)

"Captain, he found us. And has launched depth charges. HOLD TIGHT, they're going to explode."

And a couple of meters away from the U1001, the depth charges explode without causing serious damage.

"Sonar, where's the enemy?"

"Captain, he's coming back and releasing depth charges."

And again the captain manages to escape the depth charges.

"Then we sail on", was the captain's order. And again, the destroyer probed for the submarine. But then the captain makes a mistake and turns the U-boat in the wrong direction.

The Allies' destroyer rotates in the same manner, thus coming to an ideal position to blow the U1001 out of the water.

It starts sending a rain of depth charges down to the U1001. It's being shaken vigorously.

Then suddenly sonar shouts:

"Captain, I can hear torpedoes towards the enemy."

"Keep me informed and continue to sail south-south-westerly direction."

Sonar to captain: "The torpedoes are going to hit."

Sonar to captain: "The torpedoes hit the target. I hear explosions and debris falling into the water."

Captain for Sonar: "Is the enemy still moving?"

Sonar to captain: "No, they are pretty much still."

"First mate to periscope depth."

"Aye, aye captain."

Moments later:

"Captain, we are at depth. Periscope up."

The captain looks through the periscope and sees how the enemy is defeated as their ship disappears under the waves. The crew was able to get themselves to safety in the lifeboats and also helped others into their boats.

"Periscope down, we sail on."

Operator contacts the U1002.

"Engine room, do we have damage?"

Engine room to captain: "The electric motors are fine, but the diesels have been damaged by the detonation of the depth charges."

"Are there any casualties among the crew?"

"Captain, more than half have been killed by the depth charges."

"Can we still sail on these diesels?"

"Yes, one-fourth of the force. One engine is completely broken and the other one has little or no power left, just enough power to charge the batteries. So we can only continue on the electric motors."

Captain to operator: "Do you already have contact with U1002?" Operator to captain: "Yes, we are in touch, they ask if we have any damage. What should I say, captain?"

"Tell them engines broken, can only be powered by one fourth and request assistance. Operator, tell me when U1002 has replied."

"Okay, Captain."

A few moments later:

"Captain, U1002 replied. They will come alongside to help."

After more than an hour of waiting, the U1002 suddenly surfaced next to the damaged submarine.

U1002 lies along U1001 and the captain boards the U1001.

Captain: "Can I come on board?" "Permitted Captain Karl."

Karl: "Am I glad you were around or we would have sunk, Hans."

Hans: "Karl, what damage have you suffered? And are there any casualties among the crew?"

Karl: "Here is the damage report, see for yourself, the diesels are badly damaged, one is no longer running and the other is at ¼ of its power, just enough to charge the batteries. We cannot sail on like this if we encounter an enemy we are doomed."

"Karl, what is the emergency scenario in our case?"

"The regulations have been changed in view of the importance of this mission. Hitler has ordered that when this happens, we must bring the boat and cargo to safety." "And how are we going to do that?"

Karl: "We are in the Pacific and there are many uninhabited islands here. We have orders to find an island where we can hide the submarine."

Together they look at the sea charts and see a group of islands located on the Brazilian coast.

"We will sail to those, I will tow you."

They agree to sail as much as possible at night, under the protection of darkness.

"And during the day we will dive and stay still, then the enemy cannot locate us and we can rest."

"Let's first give the fallen crew a sailor's grave, then it's time to leave."

So they leave on their dangerous journey to one of those islands. The islands come into view after 33 days.

"Operator, signal to U1002 to come alongside." "Aye aye Captain."

Half an hour later. "Captain, Captain! Hans has asked permission to come on board."

"Permitted."

"Karl, what would you suggest?"

"Hans, you are going to find an island that's suitable for hiding the U1001 and after that we all leave for Germany with the U1002."

Over the following days the search continues for a suitable place to hide the boat. After a four-day search:

"Captain, message from the U1002; they've found an island with a large lagoon that can hold the boat and they are on their way back here."

A few days later, the U1002 is next to the U1001 and together the captains discuss what to do. They drag it to the island to hide the boat. While towing, both captains and officers meet and discuss what they need to do on the island.

"We drag the U1001 into the lagoon and hide it under the bushes and trees of the island. Please note that these plants must be able to continue to grow in order for them to not betray the boat. Then we will note the exact location of the island and sail back to Germany."

After a night and day of hard work, the U1001 is in place, completely camouflaged and no longer visible to planes or boats. They transfer whatever they need to the U1002, then leave for Germany as it's getting dark, but with everything that has happened in recent days, the captain forgets his briefcase with all the documents on the damaged sub.

After three weeks of carefree sailing, the lookout in the tower calls: "Captain, plane in sight."

Immediately, an alarm is given and the U-boat dives.

The crew of the plane, a Catalina of the US Air Force, had seen the boat on the radar and started looking for it. They see the boat diving but through the clear water it remains visible just below the surface. They note the coordinates of where it's located and report it to bomber command and the US Navy, find out which ships they have nearby and then sends a cruiser to the location.

Meanwhile, the Catalina switches with another so that the submarine is always being followed.

Because the sub goes further and further out into the ocean, it is decided to send bombers to the submarine. At Bomber Command, they send a squadron of six Catalina bombers to the site and begin a search.

Then suddenly the radio is heard: "Captain, we found it."

"Continue to circle above the target, we will come and assist."

A few minutes later three of the six bombers are above the submarine. They rise to above the cloud cover and wait for it to rise. After some time, the U1002 emerges but it cannot see the bomb launchers because of its height and because they are blinded by the sun.

The captain of the three bombers orders attack and they attack coming out of the sun.

Only at the very last moment do the Germans notice the planes and make another attempt for a quick dive, but unfortunately, the first bomber has already dropped its load and strikes the U1002's foredeck. The first bomb hits a large hole in the deck of the ship. The second bomber also starts its attack and again hits its target with bombs.

The U1002 begins to tilt and comes to a complete stop in the water. The third bomber also goes in for the attack. Its bombs strike the torpedo room, causing them to explode and rip the boat to pieces.

The submarine sinks completely within five minutes.

They make one flight over the wreckage area but see no survivors.

"Lookout to captain."

"Captain's listening."

"No survivors, Captain."

"Okay, then let's fly back to base."

"Report to headquarters. Mission successful. U-boat destroyed."

Three years after the end
of the Second World War

1948

Somewhere in South America on a large vineyard is a stately castle.

The owner of the vineyard and castle is Herr Frans Kohl, a fanatical Nazi. In his domain are several important figures of the Nazi party who escaped from Germany at the end of the war.

They are sitting in a meeting of the party in the largest room of the castle, where they try to recover the hidden treasures in order to start a new war.

During the heated debates, the leader of the Nazi party suddenly enters the hall. He takes a seat at the main table.

Everyone sees him enter and sits down. When he is seated, they all stand up and greet him with the words **SIEG HEIL MEIN FÜHRER**.

(According to Brazilian writer Simoni Renee Guerreiro Dias, Adolf Hitler did not die at all in the Reichstag bunker in Berlin in 1945. Dias claims that Hitler died in Brazil at the age of 95)

He takes the floor and says:

"Gentlemen, on April 22nd, 1943, two U-boats left on a secret mission from Brest. I issued the orders and I know what cargo they were carrying. The first U-boat had been loaded with gold and had been ordered to take it to a secret U-boat base on an island called Little San Salvador. We discovered this island and we removed the population. Then we started to build a full base on this island. And currently the island is fully operational. We have built factories there where we can make everything we need, there is even a shipyard to build boats and we have built a large harbor for our cruisers and submarines to dock. There is even room to moor our first aircraft carrier, and yes gentlemen, we have an aircraft carrier that is almost ready to sail. We also have an airport for our fighters and bombers.

Where that island is, only I knew. However, we have lost track of the two U-boats after they set sail, all we know is that the U1002 sunk a destroyer that attacked the U1001. We also know that the U1002 was sunk at a later time and was lost with everyone and everything on board. It is of the utmost importance that we find out what happened to the fortune on board of the U1001. And when we know that we can make Germany great again."

Eighteen years after the end of the Second World War

Somewhere near Nieuwpoort at a scout camp, after the last scout boys have left after a camp of fourteen days, the leaders are together to discuss the camp again.

Thirteen of this leadership group have one thing in common: they will all graduate this year. You have Geert as a mechanic, Wim as a nurse, Bert as a chef, Bram as a carpenter, Geert as an insurance broker, Bart as a doctor, Peter as a ship mechanic, Jeff as a blacksmith, Gust as a welder, Rob a truck technician, Jos as an electrician, Tom as a baker and Tuur as a skipper.

At night by the campfire they discuss their lives up till now. Tuur says:

"Men, since we all graduate this year I would like us to do something as a group, I just don't know what yet. Does anyone have a proposal or an idea what we could do? It should be something like a sabbatical year before we start real life, something crazy or unusual."

They put their heads together and start to brainstorm and soon proposals come up, such as 'Let's climb Mount Everest' or 'How about we cycle through all of Europe?'.

Then Geert says:

"No. We buy a boat together and we patch it up."

"Yes", says Rob, "and then we go water skiing."

"No", says Peter, "a sailing ship with a motor."

"Do you know the yard of Temse?"

"Yes, we all know that, but what's with it?"

"Well", says Peter, "my father is the boss there and he has a big sailing boat where they have to install an engine and then they would fix it and sell it. What if we buy that boat as it is now and patch it up ourselves? Buy a motor and mount it on there."

Bram interjects:

"Just a minute, I sometimes do some chores undeclared after my hours and recently I was laying a wooden ceiling in an elderly couple's kitchen and the couple's husband helped me. A little later we took a break and went for a coffee in the living room. But what struck me was that the chimney was full of models of boats. And I said to that man 'beautiful boats' and he started to tell me that he had been in the resistance during WWII and that he had brought several pilots back to England with his fishing boat. Because he was a fisherman in the North Sea. His boat looked like an ordinary fishing boat, but it was not. 'First of all, the motor in my boat was actually a motor for a boat three times the size of mine, so I had a lot of power and could leave all the boats behind me.' Then I asked him 'where is your boat now?' 'Oh well, I have a dry dock in the harbor and it has been there for several years'. If I now go to that man, I think we could already have a motor."

"Okay, great, but then Geert, Rob and Peter have to come along to see the condition of the motor."

The comrades agreed and went to see that man.

A few weeks later, the men gather and leave for the old fisherman.

Bram rings the doorbell, moments later the man opens the door and recognizes Bram immediately and asks him and his friends to come in.

Once inside, Bram tells his story to the man who is very interested and asks the question: "Could we buy the boat or its motor to provide our sailboat with a motor?"

The old fisherman thinks deeply and starts shaking his head. Geert, Rob and Peter see it and think they know that he will not sell it. The old fisherman speaks and says:

"No guys, I don't sell it, this boat has too much emotional value for me and I can't say goodbye to it, sorry, but it's not for sale."

The four boys immediately lose heart and they start looking at each other and at the fisherman in dismay.

This last one sees that and then suddenly says:

"Guys, but I have something much better for you and this is something you get from me for free."

The boys look at each other and start to smile a bit. Then the fisherman speaks again and tells his story.

"Boys, you know, here in Nieuwpoort the German occupier had a detachment of patrol boats, which were big fast boats with a big motor. Now, two or three months before the Allies landed, the engine of one of these boats had stalled. The harbor commander had requested a new engine, but it was going to take a while before it would get there. And then, a week before the Normandy landings, this engine was delivered in a sturdy wooden crate. When that engine arrived, the harbor master made a plan to mount it in the patrol boat. At that time they knew nothing about the impending invasion and would have anticipated the assembly three months later. After one week it was June 6th, 1944, and you know for sure what that day meant; after another month or more, the Allies drew closer and closer to Nieuwpoort. And the Germans became increasingly nervous and irritable.

One day, the harbor commander received an order from Berlin to prepare for withdrawal and destroy everything they could not take with them.

But I was working on my ship every day in the harbor and when we went fishing I always had some fish for the harbor master.

He gave the order to destroy everything that could not come along, including the patrol boat with a defective engine. They dragged it to high seas and there it was sunk with an explosion.

I knew the officer on the shop floor quite well and the person in charge came to me and said: 'Skipper, do you see that crate standing there with that engine in it? Unload it onto your fishing boat, set sail and dump it in the ocean tomorrow.' Since the Germans were armed, I had to obey and I did what I was told to do. That next night I went to the harbor with some comrades and we took that engine out of the crate and hid it under a pile of old fishing nets of mine. We then filled the empty crate with concrete blocks and nailed it shut again.

The next morning I was early at the harbor and then put the crate on my boat on a sliding system so that I could dump it in the sea.

Later that day we it carried out with some German soldiers on board who had to check that we dumped the engine in the sea.

And everything went as planned, the crate with stones was dumped and immediately sank to the bottom. I had the engine in my shed where my fishing nets from my fishing boat were hidden under a pile of old nets in a homemade crate.

And guys, this one is still in the same place and no one other than me knows about it.

Since I was also young and can fully empathize with your story, you get that engine from me and I wish you the best of luck with it."

The comrades were very happy with this gift and together with the old fisherman they went to the warehouse to take a look at the engine. Once in the skipper's shed, he indicated where the engine was and the boys feverishly began to remove the pile of old fishing nets. And under all the nets was a big homemade crate that they broke open and there was the engine. After 25 years, it was well preserved in the crate and under protective burlap sacks, all soaked in oil.

Geert removed the jute bags and there was the new engine, of course with some dust but still perfectly fine. He checked it, nodded at his friends and raised his thumb. The boys agreed to come and pick up the engine, thanked the skipper profusely and left.

As they left, they agreed to come and collect the engine. A week later, a small truck pulled up to the skipper's door and three boys rang the bell. The skipper opened the door and saw the boys.

"Are you coming to get the engine?" "Yes, that's what we're here for."

Together with the skipper they drove to the warehouse, collected the engine and loaded it into the back of the truck with a winch that was on the truck.

Then they left for the shipyard.

Peter had agreed with his father that they would come and take a look at the sailing ship and it was there waiting for the boys. After meeting his son's comrades, they went together on the premises towards the sailing ship. Emerging from the hangars, they came to a place surrounded by large overhead cranes, Peter's father pointed and said: "Guys, continue in that direction and you will see the ship. The boys continued and yes, there was the sailing ship. It was an old ship with three masts, one central propeller and a large rudder.

The boys couldn't believe their eyes and walked over to the ship.

Peter walked around it and with an iron rod tapped the ship's steel hull all over

"The hull is all right," he said.

Then the comrades climbed aboard and explored the ship. Everything they saw was covered in a thick layer of dirt and dust, but the ship still looked good.

A little later, Peter's father came back and asked:

"Well, what do you think? Can you still do something with it?"

Gert spoke up and said:

"Yes, we can certainly do something with this, there is only one possible problem."

Peter's father replies:

"What A problem?"

"Yes", said Gert. "I think the price will be very high."

"I don't think so", said Peter's father, "but you should discuss that with the big boss. I just saw him and told him you're coming."

The boys left with a faint heart for the headquarters and rang the big boss' bell.

His secretary let the boys in and reported their presence to the big boss, who promptly said: "Let the gentlemen come in."

Once inside, the boss asked:

"And who is Peter?"

"I am, sir."

"So you think you could just come here and buy a ship because your father has a managerial position in the company?"

"Uh, no sir."

"Well, that's good then, but I would like an explanation from you about what you intend to do with it."

"No problem, said Bart.

"Go ahead and tell me, what are the plans?"

The boys, very nervously, start their story and tell their plans in detail until the boss suddenly says:

"Stop, so you plan to take a Sabbatical year and embark on an adventure to the end of the horizon."

The boys in unison:

"Yes sir, something like that. But we have all put together money to buy a ship and we hope we have enough for this one."

"And may I ask how much you have saved?"

"Sir, together we have 2,500,000 Belgian francs to buy the boat and take the trip."

"Well, that's not bad since you just graduated, but you will have to use every franc very well. But I have a proposal for you and that is the following. That ship has been here for almost ten years. The owner, a millionaire from Brussels passed away two years ago; he was 87 years old. This man had one daughter who inherited his fortune and his sailing ship. She contacted me eighteen months ago to check on dad's ship. I could only say that it is still in the same condition as when he docked it and that we put it in dry dock. Then she said to me, 'Sir, I'm afraid of sailing and certainly at sea, and since I do not want to incur any costs on that boat, you can have it from me, provided I do not have to pay any mooring fees.' I then asked and received a month for reflection. And then I went to see what we could do with it. It was precisely during that period that orders for seagoing ships calmed down, and I thought that this could be a calm period to receive it and when it had been restored we would sell the ship. So I called back to the lady saying that we accepted the proposal. She was very happy and satisfied with my answer. I then invited her to come to the office to arrange the paperwork and fourteen days later everything was fine, the boat was officially ours.

But then something happened that no one could foresee, we also suddenly received seven orders through your father Peter, to build cargo ships for a large shipping company and if these ships were ready on time and fully met their requirements, another order of 34 ships would follow. We started on the first ship and this was finished just in time after some setbacks and the shipping company took delivery of it. Six months later I got post from that company, I opened the letter and I read anxiously (and you can read it too because I've framed it on the wall over there).

And he wrote: Dear sir, after six months I spoke to the crew of the cargo ship you built, the story of my people was obvious, the boat is all right, it is economical to use, very seaworthy and most importantly: it is very fast. Since I am a man of my word, you will be ordered to build the other ships. Signed,

"Aristotoles Pistoleros El Bonino."

Big boss of El Bonino Shipping company.

So guys, that boat, I don't have time for it anymore and since I need that space more than ever to build the other ships, you get it from me, under one condition and that is: on the sides of the ship my daughter's name must appear. You have to launch the ship Sandy 1. Can you agree to that?"

The boys looked and nodded to each other saying 'yes that's all right'. They gave the answer to the boss, but added the question: "May the boat remain here until we have made it seaworthy again?" The response was positive and they got permission, they were even allowed to use the company's machines on the condition that the boat would be gone in five months. And the boys agreed to that.

Then Tuur said:

"Sir, I have one more question for you."

"Tell me", said the big boss.

"Well", said Tuur, "we already have an engine to install, it's outside on the site on a small truck, can we bring it in and put it somewhere in a warehouse until we mount it?"

"Certainly", said the man, "I will inform Peter's father and he will say where the engine may be stored."

A planning was made with a work schedule.

Two days later, work on the ship started, Bert, Wim, Geert and Bart started to remove the grown shells from the hull of the ship and then sandblasted it to the bare metal. Once that was done, the paint was sprayed on, first a primer, then the finish in an apple-blue sea-green color. And in gold letters the name of the daughter in elegantly beautiful writing

Sandy 1

At the same time, Bram was on board with Gust to get the walls, doors and windows fixed up. This went quite smoothly as the ship had always been well maintained and apart from a few slats, doors and panels hanging loose nothing very much needed fixing and the work progressed smoothly. After that, Bram started organizing everything in the galley. After looking around, Bram called Gust. who arrived a little later and asked: "What is it?"

"Well", said Bram, "I don't know, there are so many machines here that I don't know about, what they are and what they do."

"Wait", said Gust, "we can call in Bert, he's the chef, he knows those machines."

Both men went on deck and looked for Bert. A little later they found him and asked if he would come to the kitchen. No sooner said than done. Once in the kitchen, Gust and Bram asked:

"Bert, there are many devices here from which I don't know what they are, can you help me sometimes?"

"Certainly", said Bert.

It soon became clear what was in the kitchen.

Bram asked Gust if he wanted to get Jos to check the appliances electrically and, if necessary, fix them.

A little later Jos arrived in the galley and just as he was coming in, Bram was already standing in front of him.

"You have to check all the appliances and make sure they work." "Okay," Jos responded, "but we won't sail out tomorrow so we still have some time for this."

Gert and Peter had taken on the task of replacing the motor.

First they picked up the new German engine and prepared it for installation. After that, both went on board to the engine room and found that the old engine had already been removed which saved them a lot of time.

What the boys did not know was that Peter's father had been able to persuade the big boss to help the boys make the ship go sooner, because they urgently needed that spot to build other ships.

All the work on board went very smoothly and in four months the ship was christened with the name:

Sandy 1

At a small ceremony for the christening of the ship, the boys had prepared a speech in which they thanked everyone who had helped them get things ready.

The big boss's daughter Sandy had the honor of christening the boat with a bottle of sparkling wine.

She took the bottle hanging from a rope and with a big swing the bottle flew through the air against the hull of the boat and burst.

The big boss spoke up and said:

"With this, Sandy 1 is now a fact. Guys, you've worked hard to get where we are now, sorry, where you are now. The adventure can begin and I wish you the very best in your trip. I only ask one thing and that is: come back safely after your trip."

The next day the preparation for their big adventure started. Plans were made for where they definitely wanted to go and which destination they would visit first.

But Tuur called the boys to order and said:

"Men, we first have to learn how to handle a large sailing boat and do several test trips until we are fully familiar with Sandy 1 and only then can we leave on our journey. And what's more, I have already provided a berth for us in the harbor of Nieuwpoort so that we can leave from there on our sea trials."

"Yes", said Geert, "that's all good, but how are we going to do that Tuur?"

"No problem," said Tuur. "I have friends at school whose parents have large sailing boats and they have already sailed with their parents and can therefore handle a sailing boat. I'm going to ask those men to sail with us a few times and teach us what to do."

"That sounds good", said Bert, "but what about the food?"

Gust: "You know what? I make a barbecue and we bring some meat and vegetables, what do you think Bert, can you do something with that?"

"Okay, that's all right for me", said Bert, "I'll make sure we can eat, and when we sail back into the harbor after a training trip, I'll make food for everyone if that's good for all of you."

The boys nodded their heads affirmatively that it was a good idea.

A week or two later on a Sunday, the men would meet up if the weather allowed. And on that particular Sunday, the weather was bright with a gentle breeze and the comrades gathered on Sandy 1.

They all boarded and were able to leave for their first boat trip with their ship.

Tuur took charge and everyone followed his orders.

"We will be sailing on the motor until we leave the harbor and about 1000 meters from the coast we will set up the sails."

Everyone felt the adrenaline rushing through their veins. Once they were out of the harbor Tuur followed the instructions of his fellow students. Hoist the sails of the large mast. After some searching between all those ropes, the sails moved and once hoisted the gentle wind took over the sails.

They filled out nice and rounded and the ship surged forward on wind power alone. Because the weather was ideal, they were all allowed to lower the sails and hoist them back and stand at the helm.

At the end of the day, Sandy 1 sailed back towards the harbor until about 1000 meters out they restarted the engine and lowered the sails. Bert enlisted the help of Wim to help prepare the meal. They lit the BBQ and marinated the meat. Prepared the vegetables with a dressing and Bert got the red and white wine ready for everyone.

Once back in the harbor, the food feast could begin. They all felt satisfied with the results achieved and discussed the day at length.

Three weeks the boys left again, just like the first time, but now they had to hoist the sails of two masts and everything went flawlessly again.

At the end of the voyage, the boys did not provide a BBQ this time, but an elaborate meal that Bert prepared in the galley.

"And this galley is very well equipped," said Bert. "It looks just like a kitchen in a restaurant, so all the appliances are there, even a dishwasher."

The boys repeated the practice about six more times until Tuur's friends told him:

"Captain, your crew is ready to sail alone, good luck."

The boys stayed practiced again several times but without supervision. The last two times everything went without a hitch and they felt ready for their adventure, but Tuur still thought they had to go out a few more times to get used to the routine. So they left again, their hearts full of courage, for one day, their destination Ramsgate on the English coast. Once there, they went ashore to explore the area while Bert and Wim stayed on board to prepare the food.

After their exploration, the boys returned on board at the appointed hour. The meal prepared by Bert and Wim was enjoyed with great pleasure. While they were eating, the boys discussed what the next trip would be. Tuur said:

"I have a proposal, we will sail to Scotland and we are going to moor at Kirkwall harbor. We stay overnight on board there and the next day we return to Nieuwpoort, then we have slept on board and we know what it feels like; what do you think?"

Jeff and Gust immediately agreed to the proposal on one condition, which was that they would visit a Scots whiskey distillery. The others thought it was a good idea and they made their plans.

A week passed, and the men left for Kirkwall on their first trip of more than one day.

Everything went as planned and they arrived without incident in Scotland. Once docked, Jeff and Gust left together with Bram, Geert, Peter and Rob to look for a castle. This is how they ended up at HIGHLAND PARK DISTILLERY AND VISITOR CENTER, where they were all initiated into the world of distilling whiskey and more importantly drinking this divine liquid.

Together they bought a few bottles of whiskey for on board.

On each occasion they set out for a one, two or longer trip, each trip went as it should. Meanwhile, the school year had progressed to the examination period.

With full courage and conviction that they would succeed, they set to work. After an intense three weeks they felt ready and the boys got together. Bart addressed the comrades:

"Men, we have graduated (well, I hope so for everyone) so I am going to ask the question: who has to do re-sits?"

The group went quiet and the friends looked at each other with serious expressions, until Jeff suddenly announced: "I do". A pause followed and Jeff continued: "NOT." The men burst out laughing. Then Gert followed his example and said:

"I passed."

Then the rest followed and they had all graduated. Until Bram said: "Wait a minute, I've got something."

He went out and a little later he came back with two buckets of beer, put them on the table and said, 'let's celebrate this now' and he took the first bottle from the bucket. Soon the other friends followed and the first party had started.

The next day the boys sat together again and started planning their boat trip that would last a year. Requests to sail to places came from all sides.

Geert, Wim and Gust wanted to go outside for some fresh air and during that walk they discussed the how, what, where and when.

But the comrades who were still inside were also busy talking. A little later Geert, Wim, Tom and Gust were back in and said:

"Men, we have consulted and we propose the following: We leave from Nieuwpoort and sail to Southampton as the first destination, then we continue to Le Havre from where we continue to Brest. So what do you think of this?"

Everyone agreed to the first part of the tour. Then Tuur said:

"After Brest we continue to La Rochelle and then on to Bordeaux where we stock up on drinks to be able to party, because in the end it has to be a festive trip for all of us. Then in a straight line to Bilbao where we anchor for a rest day. The next day we continue the tour to Porto with the next stop Lisbon where we stock up on supplies and fuel for the tour. After Lisbon we continue to Faro, then to Jerez De La Frontera and then to Gibraltar. Once in Gibraltar we take a few days to explore the region. Then we sail through Tangier to Casablanca. Then we go to Agadir via Casablanca, then we continue to Las Palmas and Santa Cruz where we will relax for a week. When we are rested, we continue to Santiago Praia on Cape Verde. Gentlemen, and then it happens, we make the big crossing to Brazil."

The boys all sat open-mouthed listening to Tuur until Jeff said:

"Tuur, when did you prepare all of this? That whole trip has been mapped out."

To which Tuur replies:

"Men, I spent two months putting that on paper, and I had to consider everything, like places where we can stock up on supplies and fuel, where we can drop anchor to stay overnight and so on. But when we start the crossing, we have to work in shifts because then it's sailing around the clock until we are in Brazil.

Then we sail directly to Santa Barbara do Para where we can rest from our crossing and, not unimportant, where we can celebrate carnival with the local folks."

As Tuur's finished speaking, there was a loud applause and everyone agreed with what Tuur proposed. And together they agreed on a date to leave.

The departure on an adventure

The hour of departure was approaching quickly.

The tension was real the day before the trip and Tuur had checked everything. The journey could begin.

It was mid-July and in good spirits they all waved to their parents who were on the quay wall to say goodbye. Here and there a tear was wiped, but that soon changed once they were at sea.

Tuur had mapped out the route and they left for Southampton which they reached after two days. They entered the harbor and moored. Then Tom called over the intercom:

"Everyone come to the galley," and everyone rushed there. They entered the galley and saw that Tom had set the table and prepared everything for a festive meal. While sailing, Tom had baked bread and pies. When everyone sat down at the table Tom stood up. He tapped his glass with his spoon and asked for everyone's attention and once everyone was listening Tom said:

"Boys, I specially prepared this meal for reaching the first harbor of our trip and I wish to dedicate this to all of us for a safe journey. Enjoy everyone."

They all started to eat. After the meal, Geert stood up and said: "Wait a minute, I'll be back in a moment," and a little later he came back into the galley with a large bottle of rum and tin cups. He poured a cup of rum for everyone and gave a toast.

"As the pirates have done before us, we are now going to do it for a safe sail, a nice trip and a lot of adventure. We all drink the cups dry," and so it came to pass.

The next day they left before dawn for their next destination: Le Havre and then on to Brest.

Everything went smoothly on board and there was even time to play a few jokes.

Gust was fishing and he had already caught four large cod. He called Bert the chef and said:

"Bert, here, for dinner tonight," indicating the fish.

"Perfect", said Bert, taking the cod with him and immediately cleaning them ready for the evening meal. He made cod fillets in a Norman way, in a white wine sauce. But meanwhile Gust was still fishing and suddenly shouted:

"Men, I have a mermaid on the hook!"

And everyone rushed to Gust and found that he had just caught a sea bass. They also brought this to Bert who said:

"With that I'm going to make an appetizer for tonight."

The rest of the trip went smoothly. Once they arrived in Le Havre they docked and went ashore to explore the area. But they hadn't counted on Bram who had mastered a construction worker's tricks quite well, so they entered the first sailor's pub they passed. After drinking a few glasses of beer, they decided to return on board. Once on board, the evening meal was consumed and there was still talk about the day itself.

The next day they left for Brest and as they coasted out of the harbor they hoisted the sails. There was a strong south-westerly wind and the Sandy surged smoothly through the waves.

The trip went without a hitch and they arrived in Brest. Bart had called the boys together to make an announcement:

"Men, here in Brest was a submarine base of the German occupation forces during the Second World War and we should definitely visit it," he told them.

After docking, the boys went exploring to look for the German submarine base and sure enough, they quickly found it where the traces of WWII were still clearly visible. They were given a tour by a local guide who told them absolutely everything about what had happened there during the war. But there was something that caught Geert's attention in the guide's talk. And after the tour he would go to the guide and talk to him about it. The guide was a very friendly man who had worked at the base himself during the war, and he told Geert that he had witnessed two submarines being prepared in the utmost secrecy to leave for an unknown destination.

"Apparently it was very important because the SS and the Gestapo kept an eye on everything so that no one could see what was happening. They loaded wooden boxes with a swastika burned onto one of the two subs. The contents must have been very valuable, given the surveillance that was there," the man told Geert.

Furthermore, the destination of these two submarines was kept secret so that no one knew where they were going.

"We heard nothing more, other than that one of the two had sunk a destroyer, but that has never been confirmed," the guide concluded.

After that, the friends went looking for a cafe to have a drink and later they went back on board their ship.

The following day they left for their next destination, Saint-Nazaire at the mouth of the Loire. This trip also went smoothly. It was a very sunny day with a gentle breeze as their ship the Sandy slowly slid through the water.

Bert found nothing better than to say but: "Men, I'm going to make a barbecue tonight with French bread and red wine. What do you think, is that good for you?" Everyone immediately agreed and they moved on to their duties on deck. At Lorient they went to that harbor to spend the night. Once moored, Bert started with the food. The comrades had set tables on the deck to eat there and enjoy the good weather during their meal. They laughed and they sang. Gust had brought his guitar and the men sang songs from the youth movement and enjoyed all evening.

The next day the trip continued to Saint-Nazaire. During this passage the boys encountered an unexpected problem due to a strong gust of wind. Suddenly one of the sails tore and this had to be replaced. But they also solved this together without any problems. Once the sail was replaced, Gert and Bram went down with the sail and started repairing it. There was a tangle of needles and threads, but as if they had never done anything else in their lives they repaired the sail without any flaws.

At the harbor of Le Palais they moored to spend the night. This of course happened with the necessary parties and drinks from the boys.

The next morning they left again for Saint-Nazaire.

At noon Bert comes to the wheelhouse with fresh soup for everyone.

Then they continue their journey to Saint-Nazaire. Once there, they decide to rest for a few days before sailing on. But Bram, Gust and Rob cannot resist and go into the city. After a thirty-minute walk they arrive at a market place with many cafes and the boys dive into one pub after another. Not much later the alcohol begins to show its effect and the boys decide to return on board. Stumbling little, they come back on board where they continue with wine with their comrades.

The next day Bert gets up first to make breakfast, but then he sees how the men have fallen asleep criss-cross on the deck and he thinks to himself, I'd better make a very strong broth soup, they could use that.

No sooner said than done and a little later the scent of delicious soup could be smelled all over the deck and while the men woke up they all gathered into the galley to try to eat a bit. After breakfast, the boys started their agreed tasks.

Tuur had already mapped out the next trip and they left for their next experience. Destination: Les Sables- d'Olonne.

After two days of sailing on the wind, they arrive in Les Sables, where they moor in the harbor.

It's already evening and they decide to stay on board where Bert has prepared another tasty meal. After the meal they crack a few bottles of wine and then go to sleep.

Early the next morning, Tuur gets up first and makes breakfast for everyone. Tom, who woke up from Tuur's noise, also gets up and helps Tuur with breakfast. During the preparation they talk together and Tuur tells him about a local flea and antique market that he would like to visit. Tom, who is also interested in such things, says he will go with Tuur. A few hours later, when everyone has had breakfast, Tom and Tuur set out to look for the market. After some research and map reading, they finally find the market place. The men first walk around the market to see what it has to offer. Then they go for a coffee in a cafe on the market square where they discuss what they are going to do.

Tuur who has his eye on a stand with model sailing ships, wants to take a look there.

Tom agrees and they leave for that stand together. Once they get there, Tuur looks with amazement at the models of the various boats on display. Tuur starts a conversation with the market vendor about the boats who tells him a lot of information about everything on display. Then the market vendor talks about another model that he acquired through an acquaintance. And that model would be a copy of a notorious pirate ship. Tuur's interest is piqued and he asks if he can see it.

"Yes," says the market vendor, "but then you will have to come to my house to have a look, because that ship is in my workshop."

Tuur does not consider this a problem and he asks the man for his address. They agree that he will come by later that day to look at that ship.

Then the men continue on over the market where they buy fruit and vegetables and all kinds of provisions.

After they have made all the purchases, they return to their ship and bring everything on board.

Tuur, who has the model of the pirate boat on his mind, can't wait to go to the market vendor and after a few hours, the comrades set off on their way together. After some searching they finally find the man's house and ring the bell. A little later he opens the door and recognizes Tuur from the market. He invites the men to come in and starts to tell his story.

He tells Tuur how he came by that model.

"Well, I did the long circumnavigation for years and got to know many people, including Jean-Marie, who was a Corsican, a real sailor. He had been on several ships for a long time and had visited just about every harbor in the world. On my last circumnavigation he was a sailor on the ship I signed on.

We soon had a good bond with each other and we helped each other through any problems. Until one day when he said to me, 'I bought a model of a pirate ship somewhere in a harbor to fix it, but I don't have the time for it. I want you to have this ship as a token of our friendship.' I took it on condition that we crack some bottles of rum together and he agreed. A month later, during a severe storm, he was thrown overboard and we have never heard from him again. I do have a drawing of the ship here as it should be and I sincerely hope you can restore it."

"Why do I have to fix it?" Tuur asks.

"Because I'm gifting you that ship. I am too old to restore it", says the market vendor. "And you are very motivated and still very young, you can make a lot of your life and let this model be a part of it and then it will always be a memory of your journey that you are now making. If you start working on the model after your trip, send me pictures so that I can track the progress of the repair. Once it has been fully recovered, I will come to Belgium to view the ship."

Tuur, impressed by the story, said:

"Okay, I'll restore that ship to its former glory so that anyone who wants to can enjoy its beauty."

After that the men returned to their ship where Tuur began to study the model. After a few hours, Tuur called his friends together and said:

"Men, I have an announcement."

The men looked at each other somewhat surprised and asked Tuur in unison:

"What is it?"

"Well", says Tuur, "There is something special about this model ship. I think I can take it apart to repair it, but that will be for later when we get back home, because this ship has been recreated in such detail and it will be a painstaking job to restore it."

"Quite exciting", the boys said, "but you must promise to always inform us first if you find anything in the ship." The next day the journey continued to warmer places.

Tuur had mapped out the route the night before. At the breakfast table in the morning, he spoke up and said: "Men, today we are going to sail the Bay of Biscay towards San Sebastian. Once there, we're going to watch the bullfighting of Pamplona; we can take a bus there."

After a three-day trip they arrived at San Sebastian where they took a dive in the water after mooring. After the swim they took some rest to eat afterwards. After dinner, plans were made to go to the bullfights, and they went to sleep early to leave early the next day.

At seven in the morning the guys were already sitting at the breakfast table and after the meal they did the dishes together because they had enough time and the dishwasher was still full from the day before. They cleaned up the galley and prepared to leave.

Then they left for Pamplona, taking a bus at the Miramar Palace to Pamplona via the A15.

After an exhausting bus ride, they arrived at Pamplona and went looking for Plaza de Toros de Pamplona. The boys asked a priest for directions.

"I have to go to my church anyway and that is near the plaza, go with me," he said.

During the walk, the boys asked the priest if there was a youth hostel somewhere nearby to spend the night. Together they went to the youth hostel that the priest had suggested and reserved the necessary sleeping places.

In the early afternoon they left for the plaza where preparations were in full swing for the bullfights later that day.

The bullfights started, the men were all ready and followed the spectacle from the front row. They were very impressed with the arts from the toreadors. Then someone from the audience was asked to play as toreador for a while and Jeff raised his hand and was chosen.

Jeff was led away and moments later he entered the arena, fully dressed like a real toreador.

Wim said:

"Whoops, I think I'll have extra work soon." To which Bart said:

"No problem, there's two of us."

Then the bull was let into the arena and Jeff stood there waving his pink cloth at the bull as if he wanted to say goodbye to it.

But the bull blew forcefully through its nostrils and stamped his foreleg into the ground. It caught sight of Jeff and started running towards him, faster and faster. The other toreadors tried to distract the bull and succeeded. Meanwhile, Jeff had stood behind a wall where the bull could not see him. But suddenly the bull turns in his direction and pounds with its full weight into the wooden wall, which tilts over and Jeff is able lie flat on the ground just in time. The bull is then distracted by the other toreadors in such a way that Jeff can disappear to a safer place.

Later that night after the bullfights, the comrades sat together and enjoyed sangria on a terrace and were going over Jeff's adventures.

Night started to fall and the men got hungry; together they ordered and ate paella.

Then they went to the youth hostel to spend the night.

The next morning they set out on an adventure together and went to the Cathedral de Santa Maria La Real de Pamplona, where they looked with great interest at all the statues in the church. The next day, they decided to return to their boat in San Sebastian. They took the bus again and after another tiring ride they returned to their ship. It was quite late and the men went to sleep. The next day at breakfast, Tuur said:

"Men, I have mapped out more of our journey. We sail on to Porto to stock up on alcohol. We sail along Bilbao, Gijón, A Coruña along Vigo on to Porto.

In Porto we will stay a few days to and get the supplies we need. Then we leave for Morocco and so on to the western Sahara, Mauritania and Guinea.

There we start the crossing of the Atlantic Ocean and sail to the Caribbean. So it's important that we get enough supplies."

No sooner said than done, they set off on a further adventure. They reached Porto safely and bought the stock necessary. Then they continued towards Morocco along the Sahara to Guinea where they made the crossing to the Caribbean. There, their journey continued to Puerto Rico where they made landfall in the bay of San Juan.

Once docked, Gert and Rob call everyone together.

"Men, we have sailed for several hours under sail and on the motor and this needs urgent major maintenance, so before we go partying, we first have to work on the engine."

They started on it immediately. After a few hours, Rob announces bad news:

"Men, we were lucky, the belts on the engine that are supposed to provide cooling were all broken but one; if we had sailed further like this we would have had many problems. But now we are on time so there's no problem. We will look for the spare parts here in the harbor and then we can repair everything, but as a precaution we will provide extra belts so that we no longer have to worry."

After a short search in the harbor area, the men come back on board with all the parts they need and can start the repairs.

After two days of work, they are ready to explore the area.

With the unknown in sight, they leave for Catano. After a walk, they arrive at the Plaza de Recreo where the locals are busy preparing for a local annual party.

The men there see an older man who is having trouble driving a cart in place and decide to help him. He appreciates their help and tells them that he is the mayor and invites them to the party. The boys cannot help but accept that. The next day the boys are at the appointment and meet the mayor who tells them that the party lasts two weeks, which the men like.

Then the party period arrives and everyone is in the mood.

The men sit on the table of honor together with the mayor until Geert and Wim see a group of girls a little further along on the square. And Wim says to Geert:

"Look at those girls there, they keep on staring at us."

"Wait," says Geert and he stands up and goes to the mayor. After a short conversation he goes back to Wim and says: "I asked the mayor if those girls can come to sit with us."

"And what did he say?", asked Wim.

"No problem, go ahead."

"So Wim, we are going to invite the girls together to join us."

A little later, the girls were all sitting together with the boys and everyone was extensively introduced to each other.

Gert had taken a seat next to Sandra, Wim was with Rosita, Bert had a crush on Barbara, Bram saw Maria, Geert was over the moon sitting next to Conchita, Bart got the jitters for Astrid, Peter in turn had it for Viktoria, Jeff had fallen for Anita, Gust would like to get together with Claudia, Rob had got to know Rosita, Tuur chose Carla, Tom went to bake bread for Mia, and Jos would definitely repair Manuela's fuses.

There was dancing, singing and drinking.

After a week, the men had all met one of the girls and soon they paired off.

During a day of rest from the party, they sit together at the table and talk about their adventures from the last week.

Then Bram, Geert, Gust and Tom say the following.

"Men, when the party's over, let's invite the girls over onto our boat for a cruise, a four-to-six-week cruise, what do you think?"

The others look skeptical, but then Tuur says:

"Hey, that's a nice idea, let's do it."

After the rest day they go back to the party, inform the ladies of their idea and make a proposal. The ladies consult briefly and agree to the boat trip. Then they all party until the end of the week.

A week later, the thirteen girls arrive at the harbor and search for the boys' ship, but Bart was looking around on deck, saw them and shouted to his comrades:

"Hey guys, the girls are here!"

He disembarked and approached the girls, who recognized Bart and they went on board with him.

They all sat together before leaving, and Tuur led the meeting. He thanked the girls for coming, but immediately said that they also had to work on board. The girls immediately wondered, what is going on here? But Tuur reassured them it was only regarding kitchen and cleaning work, everything else was for the guys.

The boys had taken extra provisions to make it a fun trip.

The next day they left for open water.

Tuur had mapped out the route and they headed for Caicos Islands.

The first evening on the high seas, the girls had prepared a dinner to thank the boys for taking them along. There was a gentle breeze and since there was no land in the area, Tuur had locked the steering wheel and the boat was going slowly straight towards Caicos Islands.

On the deck, the girls had prepared everything to start with dinner. The men thoroughly enjoyed the meal and everyone laughed. After a few glasses of wine, Bram went to get his guitar and once back he started to play and they all sang along. In the meantime the evening had fallen and the first couples had already withdrawn.

Tom and his sweetheart had sat down on the foreship to look at the wide sea in the moonlight and Bram's music was playing in the background. Tom danced with his girl and soon they were kissing passionately. And one thing led to another and soon the clothes were taken off, they lay down on the sails and explored each other's bodies. Then she ran her hands over his body, first his chest, and started licking his nipples. At the same time she went with her hands to his crotch, grabbed his member and clutched it in her hands. Then she started to massage him gently, she looked him into his eyes and asked:

"Is it okay for you?"

He moaned with pleasure. The same scenes took place in other places on board the ship.

This is how the boys got to know the southern temperament of the ladies.

After an eight-day trip, they arrived in Cockburn Harbor.

There, provisions were again stocked and they explored the area together with the girls.

During one of those walks, they decided to organize a big party on board for the next trip in honor of their new friendship.

They walked through Cockburn Harbor and ended up in a sailor's pub with the obligatory glasses of rum.

After some time they decided to return to their ship. When they got there, there appeared to be thieves on board trying to steal valuable things. The boys boarded and saw the burglars. They called out to the girls:

"Go get the police!", and at the same time a fight started between the burglars, who were four, and the boys, who were thirteen. The burglars were soon overpowered by the boys and got tied up. A little later, the police arrived and took the tied-up burglars. The boys inspected their ship and determined that they were just in time and that nothing had been stolen yet.

After this wild evening they all went to sleep to leave early the next day.

The start to the unknown adventure together with the girls

The next day early in the morning they cast off and chose the open sea.

Once out of the harbor, the sails were hoisted and the captain steered towards the Bahamas.

The atmosphere on board was exuberant and everyone enjoyed it.

Bram and Gert thought it was ideal to go fishing and after some time they had already caught some. A little later Bert came to see what they had caught and they proudly showed their catch. Bert took it to make dinner.

Gert, Wim and Geert started to scrub the deck with the help of the girls, while Gust and Rob set up the tape recorder they had bought together with the speaker on the deck. Everything went smoothly and in the early evening Bert called everyone to the table to eat. He had made a delicious fish pan from the fish they had caught.

They all ate together and drank the wine, until suddenly Geert shouted:

"Who's at the helm?"

"Don't panic", said Tuur, "I've locked the steering wheel and since there aren't any islands around here, that shouldn't be a problem, so tonight we're going to party like we've never partied before. And according to the weather forecast there is little to no wind; I only hoisted one sail so we are going very slowly."

After the meal they sat down together and more wine was brought out to be drunk. Then the men put on the music and spontaneously the ladies started to dance to the salsa and merengue music. It wasn't long before everyone was dancing. There was an exuberant atmosphere on board the ship, everyone was dancing and drinking. After several hours of dancing and drinking, they all fell asleep one by one.

The next day around noon they woke up slowly. Tom got up first to bake bread, he came on deck and said to himself: such beautiful palm trees and went back inside.

He went to the galley and started making the dough for the bread, when he suddenly realized: palm trees, that's not possible because we are on high seas. He went back upstairs to look again and realized that yes, he did see correctly.

He went back downstairs and woke everyone up. There was a bit of panic but Rob and Peter could imagine worse. They discussed what they were going to do and Peter said:

"After breakfast, Rob and I will inspect the boat for damage, because we are beached."

After breakfast Peter and Rob left and went ashore. As far as they could tell, there was not much damage to their ship until they came to the stern which was still partly in the water. Peter immediately spotted a possible problem. When the ship had run aground, it was high tide, now the water was going down and the rudder was partly sticking out. Peter could clearly see what the problem was, the shaft of the rudder was bent and it had gotten stuck.

With this information, they hopped back on board and called everyone together to discuss the situation.

Peter had made a step-by-step plan as to what to do:

- We have to disassemble the rudder
- Remove the shaft
- Try to restore the shaft
- If this is not possible, replace if possible

Bart and Geert, you and your girlfriends are going to look for food on the island such as coconuts, bananas, etc. You should see when you come across a fruit that you don't know, certainly not from tasting it but bring them with you. At the same time, Rob, Gust, Jeff, Bram and Gert are going to disassemble the rudder and bring it ashore.

After this was agreed on, they got ready and started their duties. Rob, Jeff and Gert started at the rudder while Gust and Bram brought out the necessary tools.

After a few hours of hard work, the rudder finally came loose. At the same time, Bart and Geert were exploring the island.

After half a day they returned to the ship with a multitude of fruits. The others had successfully removed the rudder and had already been looking for a spare shaft for the rudder.

Bert had prepared the food with Tom and called them all to the table.

There they further discussed what to do. Tuur asked Bart and Geert:

"What have you seen on the island?", to which Geert replied:

"We have yet to explore the whole island but as far as we could see, there has never been a human here, but we will go back tomorrow to find bananas."

"Bananas?", asked Tuur.

"Yes, bananas," said Geert, "they are full of nutrients and are tasty."

"Yes, and then you're going to play the monkey again aren't you?", said Jeff.

Everyone broke out laughing until Tuur spoke up and said:

"Men, let's be serious now, we have to try to solve the problem or we will be here on this island for years to come. We have no shaft for the rudder, so what can we do, does anyone have an idea?"

Jeff stood up and said:

"I think I have a solution, but it may take several days."

"Tell us!", the others shouted.

"We will look for a place on the island with large flat rocks; there I will make a fire that will serve as a blacksmith's fire where I will make the shaft red-hot and straighten it on the rocks that will serve as an anvil."

Bram said:

"But the fire won't be intense enough to do that."

"I know," says Jeff. "That's where you come into the picture. You have to make a bellows so that we can blow the fire like a real blacksmith."

Bram agreed with Jeff and started making sketches for the bellows. After a quiet evening and night they started working on the fire and the bellows. Bart and Geert left on their second exploration together with their girlfriends, Astrid and Conchita, in search of even more fruit and things like that.

Jeff and Bram had found a perfect place to start a fire. Bram started to prepare for the fire by looking for wood, because during the night he had already made the bellows, so he could start right away. Geert and Bart were exploring the northern side of the island and saw a large inlet with a river flowing out. They decided to go there with the idea: Where there's fresh water, plants grow and therefore fruits. They went through the cove and after a short while of stepping, climbing and dabbling Bart called out:

"Geert, look up there, coconuts!"

The girls who were with them shouted out with enthusiasm: "Yes, throw a rock at them and they'll fall!"

Geert was looking for a big rock and threw this with full force but he hit the tree, then Bart made an attempt and he managed to throw a coconut out of the tree. The girls that were with them loved this and also wanted to try and scanned the ground together for some big rocks to throw. They put themselves in position to throw and there the first rock of the ladies flew, hitting a coconut but it did not fall. The second lady also threw a rock but missed and it flew past the tree against the rock wall behind the tree. It bounced, changed direction, then went into the deep until suddenly, thump, a fierce metallic sound was heard. Bart and Geert looked at each other and threw a rock in the same direction and again the same sound was heard. They wondered what it was. Curious as they were, they searched for where it came from. They had to climb all the way down to get to the water. There they saw a lot of plants and trees that together formed a very dense jungle. From there they threw another rock and again the same sound, but it was very close. The tension was real and they continued. After some pulling and dragging, they saw the contours of a large metal object. Now they could not be kept back anymore and went on like crazy, pulling branches away until suddenly Geert said:

"Bart, I think I know what it is," to which Bart asked:

"What is it? Say it."

Geert said:

"I think it's a submarine from Germany during the Second World War."

They continued together and the girls exclaimed: "Be careful."

Then Geert said:

"Bart, do you remember what that guide in Brest said about two submarines that disappeared without a trace during World War II?"

"What do you mean?" said Bart. "Do you think this was one of those submarines?"

"I don't know," said Geert, "but it could be, right?"

The men decided to return to their ship and tell their story there.

After a while they arrived at their ship and called the friends together.

As they sat on the beach, the comrades asked:

"Where's it burning to get together so quickly?"

"On the other side of the island," said Bart. And Geert took the floor.

"Guys, you are not going to believe what I'm about to tell you now!" And everyone: "What? Tell us."

"Well", said Geert, "you can't believe what we have found in a small canyon where a river flows into the sea."

The men grew impatient and shouted:

"Now tell us!"

"We think we have found a submarine that is completely cam-ouflaged so that you can't see it from the sky or from the beach."

"How did you find it?"

"We were throwing boulders at a bunch of bananas, or no, they were coconuts and when they were flying, they missed and the rock whizzed past the tree, crashed into the rock wall and flew in the other direction. Then it disappeared into the bushes and suddenly, thump. We threw a second rock in the same direction and a thump again. Then we went to see what it was and after removing some bushes it was there, a German submarine."

"And then?", asked Geert.

"Do you remember the story the guide in Brest told us?"
"About those two submarines?.," said Tuur.

"Yes."

"What do you think,? That that's one of those two submarines?"

"Yes, I think so. But if that's the case, then we need to see what's inside that submarine."

"Yes, we do. We'll all go there tomorrow and take flashlights and some tools to open it."

The next day they were ready early and they left guided by Geert and Bart for the other side of the island.

After a few hours of walking, they reached their destination. With their machetes, they cut away some of the bushes and branches so that they could get through better and the submarine became more visible.

The boys noticed that the boat had been severely damaged. Then they gained access to the boat. Peter wanted to look at the submarine's engines first, so they made their way to the stern of the boat toward the engine room.

Peter was stunned looking at the engines.

"Man, those are quite some diesels and then those electric motors for sailing underwater, a fine example of German technology."

Then Tuur said: "Let's slowly go to the bow and we'll explore all the spaces."

"Wait", said Rob, "first further back, there's a torpedo room with launch tubes."

They went further back and opened the first door on board, and what they saw defied their imagination. There were still four torpedoes on board, but the launch tubes were empty. Tom called out:

"Men, do not touch, with one wrong move they could explode!"
They carefully left the space and continued toward the bow.

They saw that there were beds in the stern attached to the wall for the crew. They passed the diesels and electric motors and entered the ship's kitchen. The next room was the control room where the captain would command.

The periscope was also still present. Then they passed the spaces for the officers and the captain's cabin. Tuur looked inside, saw a briefcase and thought, I could use that, and he took it with him (he would later put it on board their ship in his cabin).

Then they proceeded to the bow and opened the front torpedo bay door. Gust and Bart shone in with their flashlights, but they saw no torpedoes, only solid wooden crates with a swastika burned onto them.

They also thought back to the guide in Brest's story. They looked at each other and simultaneously said:

"Could this be that boat?"

Then they went to the crates and opened one. What they saw defied imagination: gold bars with the swastika on them. All that space was packed with crates.

They all gathered in the front torpedo room as far as there was space because everyone wanted to see it. Geert then said:

"We can take a part of it and come back later for the rest."

"Fine", thought the rest, "but we will first repair the ship and then sail around so that we don't have to stumble around the island with those crates."

They all needed a break to recover from the shock they felt at what they had found. After thirty minutes they decided to return. The journey went very smoothly so that they were already back in the early evening.

"Men, we are going to sleep early, then we can restore our ship tomorrow morning and let it slide completely back into the water at high tide. Then we sail to the other side to pick up the gold. We first travel east, once past the island we turn north-east and sail along the coast to the lagoon, where we glide in as far as possible to transfer the crates."

The next day they all started together to perform the repairs. Now that they were all working on it together, things went much faster than planned. After several hours of hard work, they had repaired the ship. Still, the chef had again provided a barbecue, so there was extensive dining first.

After the meal they cleaned everything up and left onboard for the other side of the island.

Tuur decided to sail on motor power.

After a journey of almost 24 hours they reached the lagoon and decided to anchor until it was light again. The next morning after the meal they left for the lagoon. In a small dinghy Tuur, Peter and Bram first explored the lagoon. The entrance was very visible because it was very wide and there was almost no vegetation. After while the lagoon narrowed and the vegetation grew denser. The three of them decided together to take their machetes and clear the way, moving very slowly. Then they finally saw the submarine hidden under the bushes. They then returned to their ship. Tuur had drawn up a plan on how they would get their ship as close as possible to the submarine. The next day they went into the lagoon with their boat until a certain point where Tuur said:

"Now we have to turn the ship around. And then we back it up towards the submarine."

After three days of hard labor, they had finally arrived. They had already prepared a part to transfer the gold from the submarine, after which they went to sleep.

Jeff, Rob and Gust could not sleep and decided to continue exploring the submarine. They took some lanterns together and left. They soon arrived and opened the hatch. Rob went in first, followed by Jeff and then Gust. The men began to thoroughly search every space of the submarine. Once inside, Jeff said:

"We go to the stern and from there we start to explore everything."

As they worked their way back, they looked at everything closely without even thinking about it. Then they started checking everything and opened every door and suitcase they came across. That's how Gust discovered a fairly large suitcase that was locked. He broke it open; the other two were watching and once it was open they saw what was inside.

"Machine guns," said Gust.

"No," said Jeff. "Those are MP40 submachine guns that were widely used during World War II by the German occupying forces. But there's another suitcase, go look what it contains."

They opened it quickly and saw that it was filled with ammunition and Luger pistols.

"We should definitely take these," said Jeff.

Then they continued looking and found some belongings from the people who had been on that submarine. They decided to return to their ship and carried the suitcases on board. The next morning, the three told the others what they had discovered aboard the submarine. The rest listened with full intensity to what they had to say, until Peter said:

"Then two of us have to scan the rest of the boat, who knows what we'll find?"

They started to transfer the crates of gold.

At the end of the day, Tuur said:

"We have to stop, otherwise our ship will be too deep in the water and there will be a chance that we could sink."

Everyone agreed and they all went back on board their ship.

As they sat at the table together, Tuur said:

"Who explored the submarine?"

Jeff stood up and said:

"I explored it together with Gust."

"And what have you guys found?" was Tuur's next question. To which Gust took the floor:

"What did we find? Well, we found uniforms and even canned food from the Germans, as well as weapons and hand grenades, we also found some sniper rifles with the necessary ammunition, all of which we brought aboard our ship. There was even a chest of panzer fausts on board, which we also took with us and safely stored. Furthermore, some knives with swastikas on them and some medals from the Germans such as the iron cross and things like that."

The next day they returned home but decided to bring the girls back home first and go ashore there.

Tuur had mapped out the route back to Catano and they were ready to leave.

During the return trip, the men planned a meeting and gave the wheel to one of the girls, who obviously liked that. While the men were meeting, they discussed what they would do when they returned to Belgium with the gold they had found.

Then Jeff spoke up and said: "Men, we must also give those ladies a bar of gold, after all, they helped with the transfer."

They sat quietly for a moment until Bart and Geert stood up and took the floor. "Guys, we believe that the ladies should not get one gold bar, but each a crate of gold, after all we had a good time with them, I may say and afterwards we can come back to get the rest, right?"

The men looked at each other and nodded together: "Yes, they deserve that."

Tom and Bart had one comment and they shared it with the group:

"Okay, they each get a crate, but on only one condition, and that is that they have to wait at least six months to exchange the gold for their local money. This is because there are still Nazi spies around the world and there are certainly many in the region where they come from. We are not going to tell the girls anything until we are docked, then we call them together and tell them what our plans are."

After about three weeks of safe sailing, they arrived in Catano and moored. The girls were called together in the galley where the men had already taken their seats. They told their plans to the girls who were obviously blissfully happy with those boxes of gold, because then they could help their parents and families and deliver them a happy life without shortcomings. They also agreed to wait six months before exchanging the gold.

After the meeting, one of the girls said:

"My parents have a big cart. I'm going to get it so we can load the crates on it."

No sooner said than done, and soon they were loading their crates. Once that was done, the men took a large piece of sail and covered the cargo so that no one could see what it was.

They said goodbye to each other, which got very emotional at one point and then the girls left.

The girls decided to have a drink together on their friendship before parting. While they sat there on a terrace talking and re-calling memories, there was still a lot of laughter. The cart with the last two crates was right next to them so they couldn't lose sight of it. In the cafe where they sat, many people were present until suddenly a gust of wind yanked the sail off the last crate.

The girl immediately panicked and ran after the sail that had been blown away. But inside the cafe three men sat at the win-dow and they could see everything. They saw the crate with the swastikas on it and immediately started talking to each other. The girls did not notice but those men spoke German to each other. After putting the sail back, they took their time to finish their drinks. Meanwhile, the German-speaking men had already tak-en action and one of the three had left immediately. The others were extra alert and kept a close eye on everything.

When the girls left with the last crate, the men followed them at a distance. Once the last girl was home with the crate, the men disappeared. The next morning, it started to get light when suddenly someone pounded on the door. The girl's father, a man of around fifty years, went to the door and opened it. Suddenly six heavily armed men burst in. They pushed the man aside and started shouting: "Where is the crate with the swastika on it?"

The father knew nothing about it and said:

"I don't know."

He received a few blows and fell to the ground, where the men started kicking and beating him with their weapons. The noise had also awakened the daughter and she burst into the room, straight into the arms of one of the attackers. He recognized her from the day before and asked immediately:

"Where's the crate?"

She dared not to say anything other than where it was. The men took the crate, opened it, and then continued to speak German:

"That's from the lost submarine, we need to know where it is."

The crate and the girl were taken while the parents were simply killed by the Nazis. The girl was thrown in the back of a truck and tied up there. After an hour-long drive, the truck stopped and the girl had to get out. They stood in a large dark room with just a table and some chairs. The girl was forced to sit on a chair where one of the Nazis shone a lamp on her face. Then a door opened and she heard footsteps coming in her direction. A little later a voice asked:

"Where did you get that gold from?" To which she replied:

"A while back after the carnival party we went along with a group of boys on their ship."

"Who are 'we'?"

"Well, some friends and me."

"How many friends and where do they live?" She: "I think about ten."

The Nazi: "I need to know how many!!!" She: "I think there were ten of us."

The Nazi: "Take her clothes of and put her on the table."

Immediately the orders were followed and she was thrown naked on the table. The Nazi stood at her feet and ordered the others to open up her legs. While he looked at her vagina, he asked again how many friends there were.

She said: "About ten, I'm not sure anymore."

Then he lowered his pants to his knees, stood behind her briefly, took his penis and pushed it hard into her. She cried out in pain. While he was violently raping her, he asked again how many, to which she said:

"I don't know."

Then the Nazi said:

"Every soldier in here is allowed to rape you if you don't answer."

While he was pounding hard, the girl called out: "Wait, we were thirteen, I'm sure." The Nazi pulled back and asked:

"Do you know where they live?"

The girl was very scared and said: "Yes, I will show you."

The next day she was thrown back into the truck and they left for their village again.

After an hour of driving, they arrived at the edge of the village. The girl was taken from the back of the truck and placed in front among the Nazis and she had to show the way to her friends.

The driver followed her directions and they raided the designated home with the same force as the time before. But this time only the girl was at home. She was taken and put into the truck, then the men went looking for the crate of gold. It was then that the two girls saw an opportunity to escape. They jumped out of the truck together and ran through a maze of alleys and streets away from the Nazis, who tried to follow them in their truck. Then the girls ran to the local police station to report what had happened. They came in, totally unhinged and immediately went to the reception and started to tell their story until the policeman said:

"Girls calm down, I can't understand you."

After a glass of water, the girls started to tell their stories. They told everything about their departure by boat until they got back. The police noted everything and also asked for the details of the boat. The girls said that Sandy 1 was the name on the boat.

"But from which country did this boat come?" was the next question.

"Somewhere from Europe," was the answer, "but we don't know where."

"But what language did they speak then?"

"With us it was English, but I don't know their own language. But I can remember a few sentences such as 'ga zeggen dat het eten klaar is' and 'schat, wat ben je mooi'."

"And what does that mean?", asked the police.

"The first means: 'food is ready' and the second 'honey you are nice'."

"Okay," said the police officer. "We will first notify the other girls and provide police guards in case they come back."

The police sent patrols to pick up all the other girls along with their crates of gold.

"But first your address, please." The girl who had been raped gave her address. The policeman wrote it down until his colleague next to him said:

"That's the address where two people were killed." The girl went pale and said:

"My parents were killed by those people?"

"Yes, it seems. We started an investigation into the perpetrators. What do you know about them?"

"Nothing really, they came into our house yesterday morning and immediately knocked my father to the ground. Mother came to help him, but she was grabbed by her hair and dragged aside. Then I entered because of all the noise and they immediately tied me up and took me."

"But did you hear or understand anything they said?"

"Yes, they spoke German and they don't know I speak German too."

"Then what did they say?"

"From what I could tell, their leader would be very pleased with this discovery, but now they had to find out who found that boat and where they are now with their cargo of gold."

Meanwhile, the other girls have arrived and are put together in a large room with security at the door. Then the interrogation continues. The police officers ask their questions and the girls try to answer as best as they can. Then comes the question:

"Where were these boys from?"

"We don't know, all we know is that their boat was christened Sandy 1."

Until one of the girls said:

"Wait, I know where they come from."

"How?" asked the others in surprise.

"Well, when their ship had washed up on that island, I saw a brass plate on the back of the boat, and it said where they came from."

"And where did they come from?", asked the policeman.

"I don't remember", said the girl, "but I did take a photo of that plate as a reminder."

"And where is that film roll now?"

"It's still on the camera."

"Okay, you go with two officers to get that device. The rest will stay here."

And together with two officers they left to get the camera.

"In the meantime, I will contact the head of the federal police to report everything."

After a while, the two officers returned with the girl and the camera. The last one was taken directly to the photo lab where the film roll was removed and developed. Later they looked at all the photos together and found the photo of the copper plate. From that they could gather that the boat came from Belgium and was made at the yard in Temse.

The day was drawing to an end and the girls were all housed in a hotel that was very strictly guarded by the police.

The next day, the girls were taken back to the police station for further interrogation. But when they got there, they saw a lot of police people walking in and out. They entered the big room and were told to sit down. The commissioner came in and said:

"Bad news, our office was broken into last night and the people who had night watch in the office were murdered with a bullet to the head. Then they searched the entire building and took the file along with the photos. But they have overlooked one thing: the negatives of the photos were still hanging in the lab among the other negatives that we have already printed back. We have now taken these pictures to the capital city and when we know more about them we will inform you."

Now the police were sure something was going on and that they had to investigate everything properly.

At the same time at a secret place, the Nazis were checking all of the stolen documents. They looked at the copper plate of the boys' ship in the photo and by reading the reports from the police, they obviously knew what it was about. They immediately sent a seaplane to their secret base on Little San Salvador Island to inform the Fuehrer.

The boys had in the meantime already left Puerto Rico for their next adventure. Tuur had mapped out their sailing route and communicated it to his comrades.

Bart and Bram asked Tuur:

"What route are we going to sail?"

"Well," said Tuur, "we go through the Panama Canal and then we moor in Las Tablas."

Of course, the boys did not know that the situation with the girls in Puerto Rico had gone completely wrong.

"Then we sail on to Buenaventura where we take a break for a few days. Then we sail on to Mexico."

The men agreed, so they left.

The trip from Tablas to the Gulf of Montijo went without a hitch, and again they partied in Montijo.

Simultaneously, on Little San Salvador Island, plans were made to intercept the boys' boat, but the Nazis had one major problem, they did not know which direction the boys had gone.

In Puerto Rico, the girls were still being questioned by the police. All the girls' statements were put together and the police were able to get a picture of what had happened. However, the girls had to answer one question to which they did not know the answer, the question being: "On which island is the submarine hidden?"

The boys unsuspectingly left for Puntarenas. After a quiet journey they arrived in there where they moored with their ship.

On Little San Salvador Island, Hitler was out of his mind and ordered all Nazis in the world to search for the boys' boat.

He also sent spies to Belgium to find out where they would be.

In Puntarenas, the men headed to the city center. On their way they passed a newsagent where Geert wanted to go in to buy a newspaper. A little later he came out with a bunch of newspapers under his arm. Then they walked towards the center, where they first had a bite to eat. While they were waiting, Geert distributed his newspapers and started reading his own copy. Somewhere on the fourth page, an article caught his attention, and he started reading it. Until he suddenly said: "Men, we're in trouble."

The rest of the group:

"Trouble? Why?"

"Well, here's an article about Puerto Rico, it is about some girls who had sailed on a boat with European boys on it. And after several weeks on the boat, they had walked ashore on a deserted island after a night of partying. There they found a submarine with valuable cargo. What they found is not listed. However, when they went home with a cart with their part of the cargo on it, they were followed without knowing it. The next day, one of the girls got a knock on the door and when her parents opened it heavily armed men burst in. All that noise had woken up the girl and she went into the living room, where she walked straight into the attackers' arms. They said something, took the girl, and threw her into the back of their truck. And they left with it. The attackers who were still in the house killed her parents and moved on. Afterwards it turned out that the attackers spoke German. After investigation by the police, it turned out that these were Nazis who wanted the valuable items back. Furthermore, it says that the boat bore the name Sandy 1. the police also mention that those Nazis are looking for the boat Sandy 1 to also find out the location of the submarine. We are looking for that boat ourselves to warn the passengers about those Germans, since we do not know where they are. Guys, we are in trouble!!!"

Then Bram said:

"Is there anything about this incident in the other newspapers?"

"We don't know, we still have to check."

Then Tuur stands up and says:

"Guys listen, I suggest the following: We eat first and then we return to the boat and discuss on what we are going to do there."

The men all nodded and agreed. But then Tuur said:

"From now on, our fun trip will be a dangerous one, but we all have enough experience to complete this successfully. Let's eat now, enjoy your meal."

Jeff said: "Bert, this sure is something different to what you usually prepare," and at the same time he winked at Bert, who understood that it was a joke.

After the meal, the men returned to their ship. There were a lot of discussions along the way and after a long walk they arrived at their ship.

They immediately started the meeting where Tuur spoke up.

And he said: "Men, from now on there must always be two men standing guard on deck and we put the weapons that we took from the submarine on deck so that we can take them if necessary. We are thirteen, so we will keep watch in shifts of four, two men on deck and two inside. After two hours the men on deck switch with the men inside. This happens for eight hours. Then the watch gets switched. Those who come off the watch are given eight hours of rest, after which they are enabled again. But this is for when we are in a harbor. When we are sailing, everyone should keep their eyes open. We'd better be well prepared for those Nazis. Has anyone found anything in the other papers?"

Bart: "According to this newspaper, the police suspect that the Nazis are a splinter group of the Gestapo during the Second World War. It was suspected that these would exist but there was no evidence of this and since no one had come into contact with them yet, little attention has been paid to it."

"Okay", said Tuur, "then we know what we are up against: a bunch of avid Germans. But we will defend ourselves with the weapons we have."

Rob then said: "There will be no shortage of ammunition, we have sixty chests with bullets, we have machine guns, pistols and even six machine guns that we can mount on deck."

"All good!" shouts Tom, "but what if they come with cannons, what are we going to do then?"

Peter then takes the floor and says: "Do you remember where we got that engine for our ship?"

"Yes, we remember that." they say together, "And then?"

"Well," says Peter, "that engine is normally for a type of torpedo boat that is bigger and faster than ours. So if we start using that engine at full power, they won't be able to overtake us."

"All good, but for how long can we keep that up?"

"Our fuel tanks are large enough, usually we can sail for two months at a slow speed, so count on a month with our tanks and by then we've already entered a harbor somewhere."

And so the discussion continues, until Geert suddenly shouts:

"Stop, enough! You are pretending as if it's a game of war, but it is not, we are facing trained soldiers who know what they are doing. And we, what can we do? None of us have ever fired a gun or pistol, let alone a machine gun. No men, it seems exciting, but no. If they intercept us, and I'm not talking about the Germans but the coastguard or the army of some country, we're screwed. Because with all that weaponry on board they will regard us as pirates and that is the last thing we want."

All the friends sat staring at Geert with open mouths. Until Geert said: "What is it? In shock?"

Then Tuur said: "You are right, but what should we do then?"

"Well," said Geert, "currently they don't know where we are, so I suggest the following. We will sail to Hawaii, more specifically Honolulu to Pearl Harbor, there we will go to the Navy government of the United States of America and tell our story. Then they know where we are and I think they want to catch those last Nazis too."

"And then?", the group shouts.

"Well, then we will be able to start the retreat accompanied by the US Navy, or at least I hope so."

The men put their heads together and everyone agrees.

"We go to sleep now and tomorrow morning I will map the route to Honolulu and after breakfast we will leave as soon as possible."

The next day Tuur was up very early just like the rest of the crew.

Bert had already started on breakfast and prepared everything. Then he called the men together to eat. During the meal, Tuur said he had finished his route and that they could leave soon. So the men left towards Honolulu. They were worried because they did not know what was in store for them. But once they were out on the high seas, peace returned somewhat.

Wim and Bram sat on deck and scanned the horizon for other ships. Whenever another ship came into view, they would look through their binoculars to see what ship it was. But everything went smoothly and after two weeks they arrived in Honolulu. Tuur contacted the port manager by radio and asked for permission to moor.

Once at the quay, the harbor master George Jones came to their ship and asked if he could speak to the captain of the ship.

Tuur invited Captain Jones on board and said that they were all actually kind of captain of the ship.

Jones, who did not understand, asked for an explanation, after which Tuur told his story about how they got the ship and that they all co-owned their ship.

Jones laughed and said: "You are real adventurers I think."

To which Tuur said: "Yes we are, and we have already had a nice trip so far. But we have a big problem."

"Ah yes?", said Jones. "Tell me."

Tuur took the newspapers they had bought in Puntarenas and showed them to Jones. He had circled the articles and said:

"The ship they are referring to, is ours. We discovered that German submarine on an island and brought a large part of the weaponry onto our ship. We also found boxes with gold bars and brought them on board. But after reading those articles, we didn't know what to do anymore, so the group and I decided to come here."

To which Jones said: "That was the right decision, but don't panic, we are going to help you. Besides, with those Nazis we've got a bone to pick. But first we are going to report it to the admiral. I'm going to provide transportation, y'all stay on board here and I'll put security in front of the ship."

After an hour Jones came back on board and escorted the men to the admiral.

During that short ride, Jones said he had already informed the admiral by phone.

A little later they arrived at the main building where they got out and approached the admiral's office. Jones knocked and heard a voice on the other side say:

"Come in."

He opened the door and they entered.

The admiral stood at the window looking over the harbor and turned around.

"So," he said, "you are the men who found the submarine?"

"Yes," they said in unison. Geert continued: "We found it by chance, we all fell asleep after a big party on board and we went ashore on that island in the morning. Some of the men and also girls we had on board went to explore the island and searched for fruit, coconuts and other edibles. That's how we discovered that submarine, sir."

"Well done", said the admiral, "we knew of a submarine that had left with a fortune on board, but we didn't know where it was. We assumed it had sunk, but now it appears that you found it. So you become the rightful owner of the U-boat and its contents, that is called seaman's right. But what concerns me the most are the Nazis that are now looking for you."

Then Tuur spoke up and said:

"That's why we came here, admiral. We did take weaponry from the submarine, but if the Nazis would find us, we wouldn't know what to do."

"We want to capture those Nazis and then judge them for their war crimes," the admiral said. He added:

"We are going to work out a plan for you. Now you go back aboard your ship and tomorrow afternoon Jones will come pick you up. Then, in the name of the US Navy, I'll offer you a long lunch."

The next day the men were dressed in their best when Jones came to get them.

They all went together to the officers' mess, where they were led to a large round table.

The aperitif was soon served. At the same time, the admiral entered and went to the men. He welcomed them all with a firm handshake, took a glass of champagne and made a toast to the men.

Then they were asked to take a seat at the table. Once seated, the admiral spoke.

"Gentlemen", he said, "I have discussed with the staff what we can do for you and your safety, and we have decided the following. You will be accompanied by an escort of twelve marines, one captain, two lieutenants and two sergeants. A chef is also included. We will also arm your ship so that you can defend yourself if necessary; a military radio and radar will also be built in. During the changes to your ship, we will give you combat training and teach you how to handle weapons."

After four weeks of intensive training, it was reported that their ship was ready to leave.

"We even put it in the dry dock to determine any damage, which was a good thing, because there was a crack in the hull that we could repair. If you had sailed on like this, you would have certainly run into trouble. We have also given the engine a full maintenance, but I must say that that engine has too much power for your ship. Tomorrow we will have a briefing with the admiral and the marines who will be sailing with you. This starts at 08:00 in the morning. So gentlemen, see you tomorrow."

The next morning everyone was ready and after breakfast they headed for the admiral's building.

They entered and were immediately taken to the briefing room. There the staff was waiting for them.

The admiral spoke up and said:

"Men, in this short time we have tried to prepare you as well as we can for what's to come, you have had training and weapons' training, and what's more, you have all passed these training courses, for which I'm thankful for your efforts. Thank you. But now first things first: my officers, in consultation with me, have mapped out a route for you to follow. This route is designed so that if there is a problem, you will get help fairly quickly from US Navy ships or aircraft carriers. The officers that will be sailing with you have strict orders which they will follow."

Tuur couldn't resist and interrupted the admiral: "Admiral, don't we have a say in this route? Because we also want to visit some other islands."

To which the admiral replied:

"This has all been taken into account as much as possible."

And he continued with his explanation.

"I am going to explain to you all which route is being taken. You sail from Honolulu to San Diego, there six more marines will reinforce you, so that the total comes to twelve. From there you will continue along the Gulf of California to Mexico and then on to Guatemala, Honduras, Nicaragua, Costa Rica and on to Panama. In Panama you will take the Panama Canal to continue to the Caribbean Sea, sail towards the Gulf of Mexico and moor in Houston. The first part of the trip will probably go without a hitch. When we are in Houston, we will be moored for two weeks to stock up on supplies and fuel. Then we leave for Europe. You will then sail along Cuba towards the Dominican Republic where we will make the crossing and sail towards Morocco. After that you will sail further along the coastline to Belgium. We have finished the preparations and will be leaving at 10 a.m. the day after tomorrow."

Meanwhile, a few thousand kilometers from the boys, field Marshal Frost speaks:

"Gentlemen, we have sent spies to different countries to find that sailboat. Our battleship The Berlin (the third sister ship of the Bismarck and the Tirpits) is ready to leave. Our sixteen submarines are also ready to intercept the sailing ship. When they get close to Little San Salvador Island, our fighters and bombers will also take part in the action. We need to know the location of our U-boat at all costs."

The day of departure had arrived in Honolulu, the men and soldiers gathered at the ship. Tuur, who was already on board, came on deck and stood on the gangplank. The captain of the marines went up the gangplank to where Tuur stood and said:

"Permission to come on board with my team, Captain", to which Tuur replied:

"Allowed, and welcome aboard the Sandy."

The captain of the marines said:

"One more change has to be made to your ship before we leave."

"And what will that be?", Tuur asks.

"Well", says the captain, "the Nazis are looking for a boat called Sandy, so we're going to give it a different name and this will be: Pride of Belgium."

A final check was made to ensure that everyone and everything was on board.

The admiral also stood on the quay and wished the crew a safe voyage. The moorings were thrown loose and Sandy got off the dock.

The engine ran smoothly and slowly they left for the open sea.

The course they had to follow was mapped out and followed under the supervision of the captain of the marines. It was a quiet journey without danger, but the men did have an eye for the beauty of nature.

At one point Jeff and Bart saw some large fish swimming underwater. And Jeff called out: "Let's try to catch those", which sounded like music to Bart's ears. They took two sea rods, some bait on the hook and they were fishing. A little later Bert passed them and he asked:

"What are you doing?"

"Well", they both said, "do you see those big fish down there? We are trying to catch one. You might be able to prepare it if we have one?"

"Sure," said Bert, "bring them in."

After a few hours Bert went back to the fishermen and asked:

"And, already caught some?" To which both men said:

"No, nothing yet, but they are still swimming there."

"Well", said Bert, "try this bait and it might work", and he gave the men frozen pieces of fish. Jeff and Bart brought the line back in and put the fish on the hook. They threw the lines back out and less than two minutes later Bart called out:

"I've got one!" to which Bert, who was still with them, asked: "What should I do?"

"Grab that big hook there behind you."

After two hours of struggling with the fish, Bert was finally able to pull it on board with Jeff.

"That's a tuna", said Bert, "we will eat good from that." The marines' chef had seen everything, went to Bert and asked him:

"What are you going to do with that?"

"A delicious preparation for all the men on board this ship."

"Can I help?" asked the marine. "I am actually also a chef and I was stationed in Japan during the Second World War after dropping the A-bomb. I learned to eat and make sushi there. Man, that is delicious."

"Sushi? What's that?" Bert asks.

"It's raw fish that is cut very thin and eaten with special marinades."

"Sounds good to me, I would like to learn and know that as well", says Bert. "No problem", says the marine, "we will start right away."

Both chefs leave to the galley to prepare all that tasty food.

The captain does his inspection round with everyone and sees that everything is calm.

Around 6 p.m. the two chefs call everyone to the table with the message:

"We made a tuna buffet with rice and sushi, enjoy, everyone."

Half of the men and the marines sit at the table and a little later the next half join.

After the meal, almost everyone sits on deck and guitar music is played. After 9 p.m. most go to sleep, only Tuur and the American captain keep talking for a while as they sail on to San Diego.

When they arrive there, the six additional marines are ready to board. They cannot go ashore because the CIA has received reports that German spies have been sent to find the boat.

After refuelling with fuel and supplies they leave immediately.

The two captains follow the received orders and so they sail towards the Panama Canal.

That part of the trip goes smoothly but the US captain tells them to be on the lookout when they arrive in the Panama Canal.

After a few weeks of calm sailing, they arrive in the Panama Canal.

Before they enter the canal, the US captain calls them all together for a briefing.

"Gentlemen, we have reached a point where we will take command of your ship. When we have sailed through the Panama Canal, the enemy will know where we are, so we have to expect attacks at any given time from then on. So all posts will be manned from now on, sonar, radar and radio will always be in operation and focused on the enemy. When we make contact with a ship we will call it over the radio. At the slightest suspicious movement or action we will go into alarm.

We are now going to go through the canal, so everyone keep your eyes open and report everything."

The trip through the Panama Canal

"We sail right into the canal along Playa Farfan. Let's go!!!"

They left towards the canal, the men were nervous and kept an eye on everything. What they could not see, however, was that binoculars were pointed at them from the bank of the canal.

They were German spies who had discovered the boat.

"We must signal to headquarters that we have found their little boat and that the location is the entrance to the Panama Canal, so that they can arrange boats or ships at the exit of the canal to follow them."

They forwarded their message and immediately received an answer telling them that they should wait for a reply and follow the boat.

Meanwhile on the Sandy:

"Slowly forward marines, eyes open and report everything immediately."

"Right away, captain."

And slowly the Sandy sails into the Panama Canal without problems.

Until suddenly one of the marines calls out to his captain:

"Captain, there is a boat that seems to be following us! It remains the same distance behind us."

"Okay, we'll test them to see if they follow us."

"Tuur, increase the speed by five knots, wait, keep an eye on that boat."

After an hour of sailing, the guard reports to the captain:

"The boat lagged further and further behind, I don't think they were following us."

But that boat was indeed following them, and those Nazis obviously knew what they were doing.

A little later they received a message from the main base on Little San Salvador Island:

"This is admiral Muller, we have stationed a yacht at the entrance of the canal at Gatun in Limon Bay, this yacht is heavily armed and they will follow their boat out to the high seas, where they will board and capture them. Then they will be transferred here to be questioned about the location of the submarine. You keep following them unnoticed until our yacht takes over. End of message."

The further trip through the canal went without any problems and soon the men were at the exit of the canal in Gamboa.

Now they had to sail on past Isla Barro Colorado onward to Lago Gatun to the canal passage at Gatun and then on to Limon Bay.

Meanwhile on Little San Salvador Island where the German base is: "We put a yacht on the Fuerte Sherman and when the boat of those men comes into view, we follow it unnoticed until we are on the high seas. We will then board the boat and take it over without anyone knowing about it."

A few days later the Sandy passes Fuerte Sherman and the German yacht is ready to follow them. They let the Sandy pass and then follow at a distance of about 1000 meters.

Everything is going according to plan, but on the Sandy, the officer on duty has a look at the radar and has the captain called.

"Captain, there is a ship that is following us, remaining the same distance, I had our course changed, but it just follows us, what should we do?"

The captain arranges a meeting with the boys and his marines. Everyone rushes on deck where they meet and the captain takes the floor:

"Men, our ship is being followed by another boat, which one we don't know yet, but we shouldn't show that we are aware of their plans. I suspect that when we are on the high seas, they will attack us, and when that happens, we will be ready. Radio operator, send a signal that we are being followed and that we expect support, report our position and wait for an answer."

After an hour, the radio operator comes to the captain: "Captain, I received an answer."

The captain: "Tell me what they said."

"It's the carrier USS Nevada, they are 120 sea miles from us and can provide us with air support."

"Perfect", says the captain. "Send back that we will issue a message in due time and that we want to see those planes above us as soon as possible. Also state that they should include torpedo and dive bombers as well as fighter jets."

"Right away Captain."

And the radio operator went to transmit his orders to Nevada. The next day everything went smoothly and the boat still followed them at the same distance.

Now they entered the North Atlantic ocean and the captain said:

"Men, I think we can expect their attack in one of the following days."

Two days later the officer on duty reported: "Captain, they're closing distance."

"All hands on deck and everyone armed and ready to shoot."

After a while the yacht came into view and approached the Sandy quite quickly.

Until the captain said:

"We switch to the engine, lower the sails."

Tuur started the engine and let it warm up, knowing that he would get a lot of power from it.

The enemy was slowly but surely approaching the Sandy.

When it was a hundred meters away from the Sandy, it sent a radio signal to the Sandy saying that they had engine problems and needed help. Tuur called the captain and said:

"Okay, let's see what's really going on."

They replied to the message and called them over. But once alongside the Sandy, the Germans aligned their weapons and tried to get the boat to stop. But the captain said:

"No, we will not stop."

The Germans then fired their first salvo at the Sandy, which was promptly answered by the marines. At the same time, Tuur was ordered to increase the distance between them. Tuur gave full throttle and the Sandy quickly moved away from the Germans, but they did not give up quickly, chased them down and opened fire on their boat. The captain had the radio officer send a message to the Nevada carrier saying they were allowed to send their planes. At the same time there was heavy shooting back and forth, but both boats continued to sail. On the German boat came the order:

"Send a message to the base: 'Encountering a lot of resistance from the boat and asking for help, send U-boats and the Berlin to support us, these are the coordinates'."

That fight continued and demanded the utmost from both crews. Until the radio officer called out:

"Captain, I'm in touch with the fighters."

"When can they be here?"

"Five more minutes and they'll be here."

"Command them to attack that boat immediately."

"At your orders, Captain."

Five minutes later the planes were in sight and the Sandy's radio officer escorted them in their attack.

They dove down towards the yacht and bombed it, and simultaneously torpedoes were launched by the planes that plunged towards the yacht. There was a victory cry on the Sandy, but the captain said:

"Men, this is the first blow and there are still more to come, prepare yourselves."

Meanwhile on Little San Salvador Island:

"Are we still in contact with our boat?"

"No, all contact has been broken."

"Do we have their location?"

"Yes, we do."

"What was their last report?"

"They were attacked by airplanes, fighter-bombers and torpedo planes."

"Contact Field Marshal Swartskopf and have him come to the control room."

A little later, the field marshal entered the control room.

"Why did I have to come so quickly, Gruppenführer?"

"We lost contact with our ship after they reported that they were under attack by several aircraft."

"Did they report their location?"

"Yes field marshal, and they were sailing further towards the Bermuda Triangle."

"We will pursue by whatever means we have. Order to deploy all of our ships."

"But Field Marshal, the Graf Zeppelin 2 is not ready yet, it will take at least another month before we can deploy it." (The Graf Zeppelin 2 is the only aircraft carrier that the Germans made on their island, apart from a number of submarines.)

Two days later, the ships were ready to leave, except for the Graf Zeppelin 2.

"Field marshal Swartskopf, I take command of the Berlin (the Berlin is a sister ship to the Bismarcks and the Tirpits.) and admiral Muller takes command of the Neuschwanstein, which will sail out when it's finished. Make sure our submarines U1501 to U1507 are ready to deploy."

The search for the men and the Sandy had begun.

The Berlin left the harbor of Half Moon Beach and set out for the Sandy. The Germans knew roughly where the Sandy should be, but it turned out to be a quest on an immense sea.

In the meantime, the men on board the Sandy were very relaxed and were enjoying their sailing trip, not knowing what was to come.

The captain called his men together to issue further orders.

"Men, we were able to repel the first attack and undoubtedly more will follow. So we must be prepared for what lies ahead. From now on, the radar and radio are manned 24 hours a day. Report any signal on the radar or radio to me immediately. All weapons on board must be ready for immediate use. We proceed as follows: we have enough engine power to outrun any ship and that is what we are going to do. I also informed the central command about the attack and asked if they could have several carriers come close to us, so that they are 50 to 100 sea miles from us and we can get their help if needed."

The next few days the journey goes smoothly and everyone is relaxed.

Then a message comes in via Navy Intelligence radio.

"Captain, a message for you."

"Thank you."

The captain accepted the message and began to read it; then he shared the information with the rest of the crew.

He called Tuur and said:

"Tuur, ships have been observed coming our way, which ones they are we don't know yet, but they should be military ships."

"Do these ships not have any characteristics?" Tuur asks.

"No, they have only observed them on the radar. But we have sent out planes to identify them and, at best, we know what ships are involved within sixteen hours. But otherwise we have to be on the lookout for the enemy."

The hours creep past slowly while the crew scans the horizon with binoculars. The radar is also followed and every glance could be the enemy.

Because of the late hour, only one watchman on board is awake and the rest of the crew is sleeping. Until morning around 06:00 everyone is woken up by the alarm bell.

Both captains come together in the wheelhouse where the soldier takes the floor.

"Tuur, I just received a radio message that a cruiser and a destroyer are on their way to our coordinates, the planes that spotted these ships were fired at and shot down as they were reconnaissance planes with no armaments. These scouts knew that the cruiser was very similar to the Bismarck, so they have the certainty that it is the Nazi fleet on its way here. The Navy has been notified and these are already on their way with two carriers and a cruiser to assist us. In addition, several submarines were observed sailing in the same direction. And in order to resist this threat, the Navy has sent three more destroyers our way. We expect the first hostilities at around 11:20 a.m. We are going to prepare our ship for the attack."

The crew are all going to have breakfast first and then prepare to repel the Nazi attack.

Then the endless wait for the enemy to appear on the horizon begins.

Meanwhile on the Berlin: "Everyone on their post."

"Check cannons and put them into operation."

Then an announcement from the captain follows.

"Here the captain for all crew members, gentlemen, today we are attacking a ship that discovered a submarine of the Kriegsmarine loaded with precious treasures. We need to get that cargo back at all costs and find out where the submarine is located. We are expected to make contact with the enemy around 11:10 a.m. So everyone at their combat stations and get ready."

After agonizingly long minutes on the Sandy:

"Captain, I have contact on the radar."

"Good, warn the carriers that they should send their planes."

What the Nazis don't know is that the Americans have prepared for their arrival.

But the Berlin was able to hit its target from a distance of about 30 kilometers.

When the crew on the Sandy was still on the lookout, bombs suddenly dropped from the sky. The Berlin had started the fight.

But because the Sandy is a relatively small ship, the grenades miss their target.

Radio contact is immediately made with the Navy's carriers and the cruiser.

An aircraft carrier immediately launched eight Phantom F4 Mc Donald 2 fighter-bombers in search of the enemy. They suspected where it could be and all flew to the specified coordinates in search of the enemy.

The cruisers immediately left towards the enemy's battleship.

But with its strong radar, they could quickly see where it was and the scouts were sent for it.

Meanwhile, the Berlin kept firing at the Sandy. The bombs failed to hit and they all crashed into the water next to the boat. The shot that came closest to the Sandy hit the water 120 meters away from their boat.

The scouts had arrived at where the Berlin was and passed the exact coordinates to the cruiser. This one turned its cannons towards the Berlin and opened fire.

The first two bombs hit the sea next to the Berlin.

The captain on the Berlin was so startled that he stopped firing at the Sandy and tried to get away. But the Navy cruiser started the chase.

The reconnaissance planes were also being fired at by the Berlin, who shot down two.

Then the Berlin turned its turrets towards the Americans and started firing.

The admiral of the carrier ordered six fighter-bombers to leave from both aircraft carriers towards the enemy.

Because of all that tumult, the Sandy's crew benefited by leaving in silence to try to avoid the fighting.

The Berlin crew had seen on the radar footage that the Sandy was leaving and sent a message to the U-boats to ambush them.

The U-boats headed to the specified coordinates to set up a trap for the Sandy.

The battle between the Berlin and the American cruiser continued in full force. The grenades hit both ships and caused a lot of damage.

But then the commander of the Berlin was informed that planes were on their way to the ship. He ordered the attack to be stopped and to leave at full speed, hoping to avoid the planes.

Unfortunately it was already too late. The aircraft appeared on the horizon and they approached the Berlin at high speed.

The commander ordered to attack the planes. When the fighters flew right over the Berlin, they dropped their bombs which all struck. The Nazis fired all the weapons that were still working at the Navy jets. But then the second attack came in and once again all bombs hit their target.

The Nazis continued to fight hard to save their ship. But it was an uneven battle and they soon realized their ship was lost. And again they were attacked by the Navy's planes, which had also send out torpedo planes. These flew very low over the water and launched their deadly charges.

The Americans took no chances and launched twelve torpedoes in the direction of the Berlin.

The Nazis watched the planes drop their torpedoes which headed towards their ship. They then realized that there was nothing they could do to avoid the torpedoes and saw with sorrowful eyes the long bombs approaching just below the surface of the water. Less than three seconds later, the first hit the Berlin and the other eleven followed one by one.

The Berlin was shaken and started to capsize. Due to its high tower construction, the weight became too heavy and once past the center of gravity, the boat turned completely so that it was upside down in the water.

Then two more bombers came that bombed the hull and blew a number of holes in the hull with their bombs.

Because of this, the Berlin quickly began its journey to the bottom of the sea. Within a minute, no battleship was seen and the crew that survived the bombing had all drowned.

The Neuschwanstein crew had looked on with sadness how the Berlin, their pride, had been sent to the deep by the Americans.

The Neuschwanstein's captain was blinded by anger and forgot all the orders flying around his head. He immediately issued an order to attack the American battleship head-on. He plotted the course and the cruiser left at full speed. What they did not know, however, is that the American cruisers had tracked all movements via the radar and had plotted an intercept course.

Simultaneously, the two submarines were ordered to ambush the Sandy

The three cruisers each set their own course towards the German ship. The captain on the Neuschwanstein was beside himself, furious with what had happened to the Berlin, and he was going to teach the enemy a lesson.

But the American cruisers also came into position to take action against the enemy.

The Neuschwanstein caught sight of the American battleship and prepared to launch the attack.

After a few minutes the command came in at will and the cannons of the Neuschwanstein came to life; they spat fire and destruction at their enemy. The Americans had seen the mouths of fire and plotted a different course at full speed so that the bombs failed to hit. But the captains of the four ships had radio contact with one another and the highest in rank, an admiral on the battleship, ordered all of them to together open fire on the German enemy.

Twenty-five seconds later, all four opened fire and fired at the Neuschwanstein, which a little later took the full load and was completely destroyed. The Americans still steamed towards the enemy to pick up any survivors, but no one had survived.

Meanwhile, the Sandy had sailed on and had taken advantage of the fighting to disappear. And it seemed to work, but the two Nazi submarines had taken a stand and waited underwater for the Sandy to pass.

A few hours later, the first submarine noticed the sound of propellers in the water. To see what it was, the submarine went to periscope depth at the command of the captain and the captain began to scan the horizon.

What he did not know was that the second submarine was doing the same thing, but because of the radio silence they knew nothing about each other's position.

A little later they both got the Sandy in their sights and the orders followed in quick succession:

"Prepare torpedoes."

"Message to captain: torpedoes ready."

"Fire torpedoes two, three and four."

"Torpedoes launched."

The same happened on the second submarine, just with torpedoes one, two and four.

Then the order 'fire torpedoes' came. And with the push of a switch, the deadly weapons were underway.

But the Sandy had air support from a reconnaissance plane and it reported to the Sandy: "Sandy, there are six torpedoes heading for you, three port and three starboard."

"Sandy to scout: how far are these away?"

"Scout to Sandy: about a thousand meters."

"Okay, inform us when they are at three hundred meters."

Meanwhile on the submarines, they are anxiously waiting for the torpedoes to strike.

But then the airborne scout calls to the Sandy: "Torpedoes at three hundred and fifty meters."

The marine captain on the Sandy then says to Tuur:

"Full speed ahead."

Tuur pushes the engine open and the Sandy suddenly shoots forward; so fast that some of the friends even fall over.

Then the captain calls out to the scout and asks:

"Where are the torpedoes?"

The scout's answer:

"If you can maintain this acceleration, the torpedoes will pass behind you."

And a little later there were celebrations on the Sandy, because all the boys were standing on the stern watching the torpedoes disappear into the wide open sea.

On the submarines, the captains quickly realized that they had missed their shot and gave orders to follow the Sandy.

The submarines surfaced and started the diesels. Because of all that noise, the sonar operator could no longer hear anything. Then the order came for one submarine to 'turn starboard' and for the other to 'turn port'. This command was followed, but a little later three explosions followed on each submarine. Both boats were struck with their own torpedoes and sank very quickly, without any survivors.

The reconnaissance aircraft had observed these explosions and flew in their direction.

A little later he reported to the Sandy:

"Two submarines just exploded and sank, presumably those that fired the torpedoes at you. But since they were directly opposite each other in the water and apparently didn't know because of the radio silence, they blew each other up."

Scout to Sandy:

"The enemy has been destroyed, we can now move on."

The reconnaissance aircraft flew once more over the Sandy and then disappeared on the horizon.

Meanwhile, the captain had been in contact with his superior, stating that they were allowed to sail back to Belgium.

He went to Tuur with the order to sail home. Tuur took his sea charts and immediately started planning a route together with the marine captain.

After a few minutes consultation came the message:

"We are sailing towards Sant Cruz."

The crew hoisted the sails and the wind pushed the boat in the right direction.

Tuur asked the captain to hold a meeting in the galley with the boys.

"Okay,", said the captain, "we'll meet within an hour."

An hour later they all gathered in the galley and once sat, Tuur stood up and spoke.

"Guys, we survived the battle thanks to our friends from the US Navy and Army. We are now sailing back to Belgium and I hope that we will no longer encounter any obstacles."

Then the captain stood up and said that he has had contact with command and they confirmed that the Germans had been defeated, and that they would keep their escort until they reached Belgium.

The boys clapped their hands spontaneously.

Bert asked to speak and said:

"Men, we have had enough tension in recent days and it is time to party again. I am going to prepare a feast for everyone on board, together with Tom."

Gust and Jeff said:

"What are you going to prepare then?"

"I don't know yet," said Bert, "it's a surprise to you and me. I will discuss with Tom what we are going to make."

And everyone left the galley.

Only Bert and Tom were left. Tom looked at Bert with eyes saying, 'what did you start again man'. Bert said:

"Tommeke, don't panic, we still have enough on board to be able to party."

They put their heads together and came up with some ideas about the food, until Bert said:

"I know it!"

"Yeah what," said Tom. "What do you know?"

"Well," said Bert, "we still have a large stock of beef in the freezer: We are going to defrost it and I will make beef stew. There are also plenty of potatoes on board and we still have some strong dark beer to cut down on the stew. Those Americans are not going to know what they are going to eat, but I do know that they will stuff themselves with our Belgian pride, fries with Flemish stew, cooked the way my grandmother made it! You know, Tom, I got that recipe from my granny, and every time I make it at home, it's a party. So now we're going to let those soldiers taste a Belgian feast. We also have to make mayonnaise and provide salads and the like."

They joined forces and started on the meal.

They started to take the meat out of the freezer and let it defrost, at the same time they started peeling the potatoes and cutting them into fries.

The fryer was also turned on so they could quickly start.

After that Bert started making the mayonnaise while Tom was working on the pre-bake. Soon there were succulent scents on deck, but the boys recognized that smell and their mouths started watering.

The meat was baked with the necessary herbs and then put in a large cooking pot to simmer until cooked.

"That takes about two hours," says Bert.

Tom, who as still firmly frying French fries, also started to smell the beef stew.

"Smells good Bert," said Tom.

"Just wait Tom, it will smell even better."

Meanwhile, the Sandy sails on towards Santa Cruz with the soldiers on deck, who were, out of habit, still scanning the horizon.

Tuur and the captain were together in the wheelhouse when the captain asked Tuur:

"What are those lovely scents blowing over the deck here?"

"Well," said Tuur, "that is the food they are preparing, it is a typical Belgian dish that everyone likes."

Tuur and Bert had set the tables on deck because it was a very peaceful day and the sun was shining bright.

A while later the meal was ready and everyone sat down at the table. Everyone enjoyed eating their food.

After the meal, the captain spoke to Tuur and said:

"From today we are going back to sailing on diesels to Santa Cruz. There we stock up on supplies and fuel and continue on to Portugal in a straight line, where we stock up again on everything we need. Then we sail on to Brest where we take two days of rest and will replenish everything. Then we will continue sailing towards Belgium where we will arrive in Nieuwpoort. This trip will take about two and a half months."

The next day they left early for Santa Cruz, where two days later they moored in the harbor.

The provisions and fuel were all replenished and the next day they left for Portugal.

Slowly but surely Lisbon came closer and after a few days the city of Lisbon appeared along with the harbor on the horizon.

They entered the harbor at a leisurely pace to moor at the quay.

Provisions and fuel were brought in so that they could continue sailing until Peter said:

"Sorry guys, not so fast, the engine needs maintenance and I'm going to do that first."

"And how long will that take, Peter?" asked Tuur.

"Er …", said Peter, "two days in all, but don't worry, I'm going to do that maintenance together with Gert, Rob and Jos. You can then go into the city and have a look around. All you have to do is bring a good bottle of Porto for the four of us working."

"That'll be all right, we'll take care of it."

The next day, the four comrades began their duties early. Everything was checked on the engine. Rob and Gert started to replace the engine oil and also replaced the oil filters. A little later the air filter and the fuel filter followed. Then the drive belts were replaced. Furthermore, Gert searched for all grease nipples on their ship and lubricated them. The nipples on the pulleys of the sails were also not forgotten. Even the hinges of the doors were lubricated.

The next day the message from the mechanics came:

"The boat is ready to sail on, Captain."

Tuur then said: "All right, then we're going to leave tomorrow."

Jeff and Gust then shouted: "Hola men, wait a minute!"

"Why?" came the cry.

"Well," said Gust, "what did Peter ask us, or did we forget?"

Tuur, Tom, Bart and Geert said together:

"Sorry, but we unfortunately we forgot it."

"Not really," said Jeff and Gust. They asked the others to wait a moment. A little later, they returned with four large boxes in gift wrapping.

Gust and Jeff called Gert, Rob, Jos and Peter to come to them. They proudly handed the gift boxes to the men, who immediately opened them. One by one they opened the package and retrieved a large bottle of 25-year-old Porto.

They thanked their comrades profusely for their gift.

"But now it is time that we sail on, so men, all hands on deck."

Tuur brought the engine to life and with a large soot plume it started to move. Their ship shook a bit but once the engine was revving, this stopped and when it was warmed up, the Sandy broke free from the dock and they continued towards the open sea.

Once at sea, they sailed towards Brest.

Everyone on board did the tasks assigned to them and their journey went very smoothly.

After a calm sail of a few days, the message was heard: "Land in sight." The Sandy slowly entered Brest harbor and then moored.

Everyone was happy that they had solid ground under their feet again.

The first thing the boys did was go and look for the guide who had told them about the submarine. A little later they found him and the boys approached him. The guide said:

"Yes, I remember you and now you've returned. Why, if I may ask?"

"Well," said Peter, "do you remember that story about those two submarines that no one was allowed to go near during World War II?"

"Yes," said the guide, "what's with that?"

"Well," said Peter, "how do I put it? Hmmm."

"Come on, tell me!" exclaimed the guide impatiently.

"Well," said Peter, "we found it."

"What? Really found it?"

"Yes," said Peter, "somewhere in the Atlantic ocean on an island."

"Wow, then you were very lucky," said the guide.

"And what was on that submarine?"

"Sorry," said Peter, "we can't say anything about that, commanded by the Americans."

"How commanded by the Americans? Explain."

"Well," said Peter, "just keep an eye on the newspapers, because they will be full of it in a few weeks."

The men said goodbye to the guide and returned to their ship.

The marines who remained on board had stocked up on supplies and fuel and were soon able to leave.

The next day the engine was started very early, the bunches were thrown loose and the Sandy was released from the quay.

Their next harbor was that of Calais. Slowly, the Sandy disappeared from the sight of Brest harbor. Tuur was at the helm and steered their boat toward Calais.

Everything on board went as usual, despite the fact that marines were still on the lookout scanning the horizon. But there was nothing worth reporting.

At a steady pace, the men moved closer to Calais, passing Guernsey toward the English Channel. After a few days Tuur called out:

"Men, Calais in sight."

The men looked up, and indeed Calais appeared in the distance.

A little later they entered the harbor and moored at the quay. Tuur called his comrades together and said:

"Men, tomorrow is the day we will be back home, but we will spend the night here today so that we can finish the last part rested and arrive in Nieuwpoort fresh and cheerful."

No sooner said than done and everyone started on their tasks.

Bert and Tom started on their last hot meal on board while the rest were setting the table.

After an hour and thirty minutes, the meal was ready and everyone sat at the table. During the meal, Tuur spoke to the captain of the marines and they discussed what was to happen the next day. But he said to Tuur:

"Our arrival has been reported and your family is aware of our arrival. Even the consul of the United States of America will attend. The Belgian government has also been informed and they will also be there."

That night everyone went to bed in time to leave early the next morning.

The first alarm clock went off at five the next morning. It was Tom's, who got up quickly, refreshed himself, then went to the galley.

Tom had prepared everything the day before to make dough for bread and by seven o'clock the first loaves had been in the oven for a while.

Bert, who got up an hour after Tom, had already prepared breakfast and set the table. At about half past seven a general alarm signal was given and everyone was tossed out of bed. Then Tuur announced:

"Everyone at the table at eight o'clock, washed and shaved."

And at eight o'clock they were all at the table.

Then Bert came in with a large dish of bacon and eggs. Tom's bread was ready and sliced on the table. Everything was freshly made and smelled delicious. The aroma of the fresh coffee also tickled everyone's noses.

The men sat down at the table and after a short prayer of thanksgiving they began to eat.

Together they discussed the reunion with their parents, families, friends and acquaintances. And the emotions slowly began to take over. After being away from home for a long time, the prospect of seeing everyone again was quite emotional.

But they did not let their feelings be known and continued to eat quietly.

After the meal, the engine was started. Once warmed up, the bunches were thrown loose and the Sandy left for the wide-open sea for the last part of their journey.

After a few hours they approached Nieuwpoort, and to everyone's surprise they were welcomed by pleasure boats from people who had followed everything through the media.

Under a large escort and with loud honking, they were brought into the harbor of Nieuwpoort.

When the men were almost at their berth, they saw for the first time the size of the reception committee. There was even a fanfare that was playing the Brabançonne.

They moored and the gangplank was laid out. Tuur went ashore first and was welcomed by his parents, but immediately afterwards representatives of the government, the American consul and officers of the Belgian and American army welcomed them. Even people from national TV were present. They captured everything on film. The print press was fighting to be the first to publish their story.

The rest of the men had also gone ashore and the press also stormed them.

One by one they were interviewed and told their stories.

In great color and detail they all related what they had experienced on their journey; the adventures, the discovery of the submarine, its cargo and the chase by the Nazis. The battles that were fought and won thanks to the help of the American Army, Navy and Airforce.

Then the mayor invited the boys to come to the town hall.

The gendarmerie, who was also present to ensure that everything proceeded according to the law, would make an inventory of what the men had on their hands.

And at the same time they kept watch until they returned from the town hall.

After being received by the mayor, the men had returned to their boat, where the gendarmerie had completed their inventory and handed the ship back to the boys.

"Well," said Geert, "we will first arrange a meeting to see what we will do with the cargo, we cannot leave it on board our boat."

"Wait!" said Wim. "My father is the manager of a local bank. I will ask if we can put the gold in their safe."

No sooner said than done and the cargo was transported from the boat to the bank where it was placed in the safe.

The necessary documents were drawn up with the number of crates of gold in the safe. The safe was closed so that the men could go to their parents without any worries.

They agreed to come back on board the next day to sort everything out and clean up the boat.

At about seven o'clock in the morning, Tuur arrived on board, thinking he would be the first, but no, he entered the galley and the smell of fresh coffee tickled his nose. Everyone was already present. They sat together as had happened so many times during their trip and reminisced about their trip.

They talked like that until noon, until Gust said:

"Men, I'm going to leave you now, but we'll still hear from each other."

Everyone said goodbye and left with a satisfied feeling. But not before they had agreed to make another trip.

You can also buy this book in Dutch.

ISBN: 978-3-99131-103-4
www.novumpublishing.nl

HERZ FÜR AUTOREN A HEART FOR AUTHORS À L'ÉCOUTE DES AUTEURS MIA KAPΔIA ΓIA ΣYΓΓΡ
RTA FÖR FÖRFATTARE UN CORAZÓN POR LOS AUTORES YAZARLARIMIZA GÖNÜL VERELIM SZÍ
ORE PER AUTORI ET HJERTE FOR FORFATTERE EEN HART VOOR SCHRIJVERS TEMOS OS AUTC
ÖINKÉRT SERCE DLA AUTORÓW EIN HERZ FÜR AUTOREN A HEART FOR AUTHORS À L'ÉCOU
ΑÇÃO ВСЕЙ ДУШОЙ К АВТОРАМ ETT HJÄRTA FÖR FÖRFATTARE Á LA ESCUCHA DE LOS AUTOR
EURS MIA ΚΑΡΔΙΑ ΓΙΑ ΣΥΓΓΡΑΦΕΙΣ UN CUORE PER AUTORI ET HJERTE FOR FORFATTERE EEN
ARLARIMIZA ... SER ... ÖINKÉRT SERCE DLA AUTORÓW EIN HERZ FÜ
SCHRIJVERS ... OS ... AÇÃO ВСЕЙ ДУШОЙ К АВТОРАМ ETT HJÄRTA FÖ

The author

Herman Mertens was born in Geel, Belgium, on April 22nd, 1959. His youth was carefree, full of adventure and imagination, a spirit that is reflected in his writings.

Following his studies for a professional bachelor's degree he joined the Federal Police force. However, he has never lost his love of adventure and still enjoys cycling holidays in the Ardennes region. He loves good food and cooking, as well as music and plays the drums in the musical group The Lary's. He often entertains his family with is storytelling skills and is known as 'the family storyteller'. Herman Mertens has had a lifelong interest in submarines, a fascination which resulted in his first book De verloren Duitse duikboot (The Lost German Submarine), in which he brings his own 'twist' to the Second World War.

Mertens is divorced and has two daughters.

The publisher

*He who stops
getting better
stops being good.*

This is the motto of novum publishing, and our focus
is on finding new manuscripts, publishing them and
offering long-term support to the authors.
Our publishing house was founded in 1997, and since
then it has become THE expert for new authors and
has won numerous awards.

**Our editorial team will peruse each manuscript
within a few weeks free of charge and without
obligation.**

You will find more information about
novum publishing and our books on the internet:

w w w . n o v u m - p u b l i s h i n g . c o . u k